The itsy bitsy spider went up the waterspout…

Down came the rain and washed the spider out…

Up rose the sun and dried up all the rain…

And the itsy bitsy spider was out to kill again!

Deadly Rhymes

A lullaby was never so twisted...
...or so deadly!

Cory Blystone

Kwirk Publishing
Vancouver

Why are you reading this? There is nothing of importance here! Nothing at all! Unless, of course, you want to be one of those people who literally read a book from cover to cover, then, I suppose, you are forgiven.

This is a book. Duh.

For my Grandma Flo. Your life, stories, and support have inspired me more than you'll ever know.

To Brandon. Thanks for all the ideas!

And to Greg. Without you, I never would have realized my dreams, or my potential.

Deadly Rhymes

Chapter 1
A Creak from Down Below

Violently waking from a nightmare reliving a recent attack, Sheree found herself mere inches away from a viscous loogie about to fall into her open mouth. That's when she decided it was finally time to kill her little brother. Nine years was long enough to ruin her life, and nine years was all the life he was going to get.

"Get out of my room Brendon!" Sheree screamed from her bed, throwing a round purple pillow in his direction but missing him by a long shot, with the pillow instead hitting a framed picture on her nightstand, knocking it onto the floor. The glass pane had shattered years ago leaving just the outer frame, so any hope of stray shards hitting her brother were also out of the question, much to Sheree's dismay.

"Brendon, leave your sister alone," Mrs. Hollins yelled from the bottom of the stairs, a wooden spoon dripping with blood red sauce in her hand as if she was threatening her son with it.

Brendon rolled his eyes and spun around. "Oh all right. Geez!"

A pleased smile was over Sheree's face as she watched her brother leave the room. Getting him in trouble was always a pleasure because for years she was an only child, spoiled rotten to the core. Veruca Salt had nothing on her. That is, until little Brendon came home from the hospital that fateful day nine years ago, completely crushing Sheree's worldview that life revolved around her. It was a devastating blow to her fragile little-girl ego, and one she has never quite been able to forgive. For all the affection once bestowed upon her was now even more-so given to this boy. This strange, lumpy, wriggly little monkey her parents called Brendon, the boy. And they always added that part about him being a boy to friends and family as if having a penis was something to be proud of! With a bit of satisfaction, and also a bit of frustration at having to get up, she walked over to the pillow she threw at Brendon and tossed it back onto her bed.

It was the last day of August 1999 and everyone was obsessed with the world ending. Sheree on the other hand was more concerned about the end of her privacy.

The Hollins family had just moved into an old house on Song's End in the little town of Ravenwood a few weeks prior. It was at least a hundred years old, if not older. However, the 'recent' remodel added some much needed bathroom space and amenities, albeit, almost entirely in a putrid shade of avocado green. Avocado wasn't much of a big thing to Sheree because it was her favorite fruit to eat, and a great moisturizer that also helps to maintain an even skin tone. Her father said they would remodel next summer, while her mother's response to that was that it would never happen unless she did it herself. Other than the few odds and ends and minor patches to be made, the house was great. With the exception of rumors around town that the house was haunted and that was why the last family moved. Of course, rumors around town also said that the entire street was haunted, so obviously these small-town folk have nothing better to do than tell ghost stories, or so Sheree thought.

The Hollins's daughter Sheree was tall and thin, but not so thin you could bend her over your knee and snap her in half. There was a little pudge in her mid-section that she called her 'papa belly' after her grandfather on her dad's side. "It's all his fault!" she proclaimed to a friend one day, "Damn genes are too strong, it will never go away!" While she persisted that it was indeed hereditary, it was also a possibility that her late night infatuation with Death by Chocolate ice cream may have partially contributed to it as well. Her eyes were an almost unreal aquamarine, shimmering like the deep blue sea somewhere tropical and warm and definitely not Washington State, and she also had wavy strawberry blond hair that flowed just below her shoulders, which she normally had pulled into a ponytail that at the moment was being strangled by the purple pillow. For the past few weeks she had been trying to decide whether or not to bleach out the reddish tint and just go blond.

Although she was sixteen years old, she was only a freshman in high school. She started school a year late due to an early childhood tragedy, and then had to take first grade twice because she was afraid to cross the street to get to the bus stop and would go into convulsions and miss school and thus not be in class enough to learn anything. One thing Sheree didn't like was that she was going to be twenty years old before she graduated, but being the only driving freshman was sure to make her popular. And if there was one thing Sheree liked, it was to be popular. In middle school, back when they still lived in West Seattle, she was an excellent gymnast and head of the cheerleading team. Although she had only been to Ravenwood High for a week, she was quickly becoming an A-lister among people to hang out with, even with the upper classmen.

Brendon was in complete contrast to his sister. He was a little short for his age, and a little stocky, and his hair and eyes were both a light brown. And while he would appear sweet and innocent on the outside, those who were familiar with the kid knew that he always had something up his sleeve. He also, for some reason or another, would wear over-the-calf socks pushed all the way down to his ankles, leaving the bulk of the sock flopping around in front of his toes. Sheree had always hoped that this would cause him to trip, fall, and break his head open, possibly indirectly causing a frontal lobotomy, leaving behind a more agreeable little brother. Of course, this never happened. Brendon seemed quite adept at wearing his socks, even if it was rather goofy looking.

"Dinner time!" Mrs. Hollins called from the kitchen.

Hungrier than she realized, Sheree rushed out of her room and jogged down the old staircase. Each step was followed by a small creak from the ancient wood, the first few causing her to wince even though she knew to expect them. As she looked forward, turning her head toward the dining room table, she saw her brother sitting in her usual spot.

"What do you think you're doing?" she questioned Brendon, giving him a cold stare as she walked over to the table, arms folded across her ample chest.

Brendon just looked up at his teenage sister with an evil grin across his round face. Too evil.

"Oh, sit in another chair. There are plenty of other places to sit at this table," Mr. Hollins, their young looking father told Sheree. He may have been forty-one, but he looked like he was only in his twenties. A lot of her friends would mistake him for an older brother and ask if he was seeing anyone, that is, until they'd see him drinking thick, dark beer and watching the television as if it were a god, then he was obviously just her dad. Or so she convinced herself, never acknowledging the fact that most of her friends would still have sex with him knowing full well his real age.

Reluctantly, she sat next to Brendon in his usual spot. *He's going to pay,* Sheree thought to herself, staring at him with eyes full of anger, her cheeks and ears flushing with red. *He always gets his way. Why do they let him get away with everything? Oh, that's right… he's 'the boy.' Goddamned penis.*

Sheree decided to push the subject off to the side, landing in the 'To Be Continued' portion of her brain, which, at the moment, looked like a disarrayed scattered mess right next to an overflowing trash bin. All bad thoughts aside, she was ready to enjoy the meal.

Mrs. Hollins, with her flashy copper hair that obviously came from a cheap box of generic brand hair dye found at the supermarket, came into the dining room carrying a platter of spaghetti. She set the plate down in the center of the large oak table for eight and sat herself down in the chair next to her husband.

Brendon slid his plate over to the spaghetti dish and scooped himself a large helping of the pasta, some of the sauce splashing here and there as he did so, marking the table with what looked like blood splatter from a crime scene. There was a look of disgust over Sheree's face as she watched her brother slurp down the noodles, tomato sauce clinging to his cheeks, nose, and chin. His tongue unsuccessfully tried to lick it off his face, inadvertently smearing what appeared to be even more spaghetti sauce around his lips. He looked like a clown and the sad thing was that Sheree knew that he enjoyed it. Both Mr. and Mrs. Hollins had already served themselves and started eating their dinner. It was silent except for the chewing mouths and clinking of milk and wine glasses being placed back on the table, so really it sounded more like feeding time at the pig farm minus the oinking.

"Oink, oink!" Brendon oinked.

"Thank you, Brendon," Mrs. Hollins responded. "I also think we have a winner with that new Ragu sauce. Don't you agree Frank?"

"Oink!" Mr. Hollins said, too.

Rolling her eyes and coming to the realization that her family was a bunch of pigs, Sheree reached over to the spaghetti platter and put a small pile onto her plate and began picking the mushrooms out with a fork. *I hate mushrooms,* she thought, making an annoyed face as she continued moving the fungus off to the side of her plate and allowing one to quite noticeably fall onto the table. *So much for your winning spaghetti sauce theory, Mother.*

As if Mrs. Hollins had read her daughter's mind, she suddenly realized the fungal catastrophe she had created. How could she have just forgotten that Sheree hated mushrooms? She had hated them since being introduced to solid foods in her infancy. But she brushed it off because the rest of the family obviously loved them, and, well, she also knew that Sheree was just so complacent about everything that she could practically get away with murder and Sheree wouldn't say anything about it one way or another. After having mentally worked through her little dilemma, she smiled and continued eating dinner, twirling another bite of spaghetti with her fork, topping it off with a huge, slimy, whole mushroom.

Once they were finished eating, Mr. Hollins got up, wiped his chin of any sauce that was still on his face, then went into the family room and turned on the television. The same ritual he did every night. With the exception of Saturday night, that is. On Saturday's he would get up out of his chair, give his wife a kiss, and then softly stroke her hair before heading into the family room to watch the TV. This, Sheree thought, must be their little code for, "After I'm done watching three hours of mindless bullshit, let's go into the bedroom and fuck." Just the thought of her parents actually having had sex at least twice to conceive her and her brother was revolting enough, let alone them doing it on a regular basis.

Thinking to herself what album she was going to listen to—another nightly ritual—Sheree got up and was about to go back to her room when her mother told her that she had kitchen duty first.

"Mom, it's Brendon's turn tonight," she complained, hoping that she'd somehow get out of it.

Her mom glared at her with a don't-argue-with-me look. "I don't think so. Brendon did it last night."

Recognizing her defeat and realizing she caved far too quickly than she normally would have, Sheree scrambled over to the table and began clearing it off, not even caring that the mushroom that fell off her plate and onto the table was now on the floor, putting the dishes directly into the dishwasher without rinsing them off first, mumbling nondescript curses. She knew that the job wasn't hard, and it didn't take very long, but she still hated doing it every other night. Maybe if there were five more kids and she only had to do it once a week she'd be happier. But then the thought of six Brendons would pop into her mind and rid her of all wishes for more siblings. When she finished the five-minute task, she strolled over to the stairs.

CREAK!

Sheree turned her head toward the basement door, then she looked back to the family room where her parents were; her dad staring blankly at the television as if he was under hypnosis, and her mom reading one of those magazines that only older women and gay men read. *Maybe it's just the house, she thought. Old houses always make noises for no reason, right?*

CREAK!

Hmm, she thought. *Maybe it's Brendon.*

Getting a wicked look on her face, she went closer to the door… closer, almost there now. She reached for the doorknob and turned it. The iron door hinges creaked with a shrilling sound, causing her dad to momentarily flinch but not enough to break him out of the trance that was holding him hostage to the television set. Her mother on the other hand probably didn't even hear it, too absorbed in some article about creating an inexpensive duvet cover out of two flat sheets, or embroidering monograms on napkins or something absurd like that. Or maybe it was the three glasses of red wine with dinner she swallowed down like a fish that altered her sensory reactions. Entering the basement, she searched for the light switch, looking furiously to locate it. There didn't seem to be one as she felt over the walls on either side of the door. *There has to be a switch somewhere,* she said to herself, frustrated. Deciding that the light from the hall was good enough, she took a precautious step down the stairway that led to the dark, unwelcoming, musty room below the house.

SLAM!

Total darkness.

Terrified, Sheree became panic-stricken from the darkness in the horrifying subterranean chamber and reached for the doorknob, turning it but it wouldn't turn. Trying again with a little more force, thinking that it was just old and maybe rusted, hoping it would budge if she put a little strength into it.

Still nothing.

It was pitch black, not even a sliver of light from between the bottom of the door and the floor, as if it had been sealed. Turning her head from side to side and carefully behind her in hopes that she would find a source of light somewhere, but not daring to move her feet for fear that she would stumble down the stairs.

Tumble.

Break her neck.

Die.

Or worse, become paralyzed.

There was nothing but desolate blackness surrounding her. The air seemed to be getting heavy like she was going to pass out, so she banged her hands on the door over and over.

"Help!" she cried, breathing ferociously. "Let me out!"

The door burst open, intense light pouring in and washing everything out momentarily. Shielding her eyes with her arm, she looked down, and there on the ground, Sheree saw her little brother laughing hysterically, holding his stomach from the pain.

That's it! I can't take it any longer. He's going to pay big time!

Staring at Brendon for a moment she decided that he wasn't worth it. Although she felt like beating the crap out of him, she instead gave him a light kick to his side then stormed up the steps to her bedroom, hot tears starting to slide down her cheeks. It was the only somewhat private place in the house (though she wished it had a lock) she could be that didn't give her the creeps or scare her. Barely audible from top of the stairway she heard her father tell Brendon to stop laughing because he was watching a very important TV show about some war and he'd understand when he got older how important it was for him to watch it.

How could he do that to me? He knows that I can't stand being locked up in a dark room, especially not after...

Once again, she pushed the angst toward her brother aside, bottling it up. After she got into her room, she slammed the door shut and turned the stereo on, raising the volume loud enough for the whole house to hear clearly. She turned it down soon after, knowing that she would get in trouble from her dad if he couldn't hear the TV show about some war that she was far too young to understand the importance of. She decided to dig out her old headphones so she could listen to it as loud as she wanted. Placing the headphones on and letting out a loud breath, she drifted off into her own little world, escaping all of her problems.

Chapter 2
The Itsy Bitsy Spider...

Sheree was sleeping when she heard a faint noise, one she had never heard before. Still not quite awake, she tried to concentrate on where the sound was coming from. Listening more intently, she got up from her bed and walked around, making loud creaks from the aged floorboards. Trying to figure out where the sound was coming from, she turned toward the air vent. After a few seconds, she realized the sound was indeed coming from the vent. Walking slowly around her bed, over the hardwood floors to the vent cut out next to the wall, she reached over to her bedside lamp and turned it on to illuminate the room. The brightness of the light blinded her for a few seconds, causing her to close her eyes and blink in rapid succession until they became used to it. Getting down on her hands on knees, she leaned in closer and put her ear to the air vent and listened, hoping she could make out what the sound was.

"The itsy bitsy spider went up the waterspout..."

Sheree listened closer. She knew it was Brendon. It had to be. He was trying to scare her again.

"Down came the rain and washed the spider out…"

The voice however was not of Brendon's. It was too young, maybe from a three or four year old.

"Up rose the sun and dried up all the rain…"

She listened more intently, trying to conclude who was singing the song. And why?

She pressed her ear as close to the vent as she could.

"And the itsy bitsy spider was out to kill again!"

Suddenly a warm blast of air flew up from the vent. Quickly, Sheree lifted her head and moved away. The automatic heating had turned on. Jumping onto her bed, she realized that she was too frightened to go back to sleep, so she grabbed the remote control and turned on her TV. She turned the volume down so that nobody else would hear it. All night, she watched old reruns of the classics. Thank God for TV Land.

The next morning, Brendon descended from the staircase slowly. Sheree and the rest of the family were already in the kitchen getting ready to eat breakfast.

"I heard voices last night, Mom. I could hardly sleep," Brendon said with a tired speech, wiping his eyes. His short hair was all out of place as if it were wind-whipped after a day of swimming at the beach.

Could it be true? Could Brendon have also heard the dreadful singing that was coming from the vent the night before?

"It sounded like Mr. Ed," he informed everyone, sitting down on the empty stool at the kitchen's breakfast bar with the others.

Sheree's heart sank. That was one of the shows that she had watched when she couldn't sleep.

Oh well. So I was the only one that heard the singing. Should I tell anyone? Or should I keep it to myself?

After she filled her bowl with cereal, she poured milk into it because that is what has done since the dawn of grain-based cold cereal's invention. Spooning the cereal down, she made sure to cover all of the dry nuggets before she began eating. The spoon seemed to wiggle as she picked it up from the bowl. She had already taken a couple bites before and didn't notice the wiggle. Then something caught her eye. More than curious, she lifted the spoon towards her and screamed. Dropping the spoon back into the bowl, milk spraying around it, she pushed herself back and stood up.

The rest of the family looked at Sheree, wondering what all of the ruckus was about. The shear shrillness of her shriek caused Mrs. Hollins to jump from her seat and almost choke on a granola cluster.

A frightened expression was on Sheree's face as she looked at the contents in the spoon and bowl. Frantically she began digging in her mouth, hoping she hadn't swallowed any.
Both Mr. and Mrs. Hollins glared at their son accusingly.

"That's not very funny, Brendon."

"Me? You think that I put spiders in her cereal?" Brendon asked, shocked that his parents would think he would pull a prank like that in front of them. "It wasn't me! I swear!"

Sheree was too sickened to finish eating and ran upstairs to get ready for school. Somehow, she believed Brendon. It was the look in his eyes that told her he was telling the truth. However, she saw that look in his eyes so rarely, that it was possible she had misread them. After taking off her nightshirt, she changed into a maroon top and a pair of tight-fitting faded blue jeans.

Guilty feelings ran through her head for letting her brother get in trouble for something he didn't do. But not for long.

No, he deserves it. Maybe this will stop all of his pranks that he always plays on me, she thought, trying to convince herself that it was all for the better. Some spare-the-rod-spoil-the-child-insane-troll-logic she'd read about somewhere. Just then, she almost wished her parents had a rod for beatings, but quickly flushed that thought down the toilet of her imagination when she thought about it more clearly as it would also have been used on her for acting out of line.

Rushing out of her room, she bumped into Brendon about to enter his. A pathetic look was over him. She had never seen her brother look so down before. "I know that you didn't do it Brendon," she said to her brother reassuringly. "A house like this is probably infested with all kinds of disgusting creatures. I mean, you live here after all."

"You wanna tell Mom and Dad that? Maybe it'll get me out of trouble," Brendon suggested, giving a little smile that someday will make all the girls swoon.

Without any control, her body wriggled and her eyes began twitching and her hands waved in front of her as if his suggestion was the most preposterous thing she had ever heard. "Hell no! What are you, crazy? You never get disciplined! You're taking this one whether you did it or not!"

A scowl and low growl escaped from Brendon as he turned to enter his bedroom.

"If you hurry, I'll give you a ride to school," she told him before he closed the door.

His scowl became a wide smile when he heard this, for if there was one thing he hated more than anything it was walking to school, even though it was practically just across the street. Well, across the street and through the trail that led to Storybook Lane, which only had three structures on the entire street: Ravenwood Elementary, Ravenwood Middle School and the Ravenwood Public Library.

CREAK!

This house gives me the creeps.

Feeling a little adventurous, especially after evading accidental tiny black spider ingestion, Sheree put her rear on the rail and started sliding down it. The wind rustled through her hair as she flew down the handrail of the old staircase.

She heard another creak.

Then a crack.

Two more cracks.

Suddenly she slipped off of the rail and tumbled down the steps. She tried to put her arms over her head to protect it but they just kept flopping around uselessly. Spinning around and around, she wondered if the dizziness and the pain would ever stop.

THUD!

Finally hitting the floor, Sheree turned herself onto her back and looked up toward the railing. There she saw that three of the posts on the handrail were broken, split in half.

Her terrified parents ran to her side.

"Are you alright? What happened? Does anything feel broken? Should we call a doctor? How many licks does it take to get to the Tootsie Roll center of a Tootsie Pop?"

The questions seemed endless and the last one didn't make sense, as Sheree sat up and kept staring at the steps. It was possible that she made the Tootsie Pop one up in her head, but in all the confusion she wasn't sure.

"I feel fine. My elbow hurts a little, but nothing feels broken," she assured her mom and dad who continued to touch her in places that would make most teenagers cringe while standing up.

A few loud thumps could be heard upstairs as Brendon ran out of his room to see what the loud thud was that he heard from his bedroom while he was putting his pants on. At the bottom of the steps, he saw his sister, and then he noticed the broken posts of the handrail.

Still in shock from the incident, she slowly placed herself on the loveseat in the living room by the staircase, moving a piece of wood that had fallen so she could sit. Her parents had disappeared, probably finishing getting ready for work. It seemed that Brendon had gone back to his room or possibly the bathroom.

What happened? Why did I suddenly spring from the railing?

Sitting on the couch, she tried analyzing the event over and over again in her head, but kept coming to the same illogical conclusion. *It was like I was... pushed.* She shook her head and got up from the sofa, thinking that being pushed by an invisible force was just crazy talk. Reaching into her purse that was sitting on the end table next to the loveseat, she felt around for her hand mirror to look at herself.

"Ouch!" she yelled, lifting her hand out of the purse and seeing that the mirror was broken. A small piece of glass had lodged itself into the palm of her hand, so she pried it out with her fingernails as she walked into the kitchen. Wiping the blood off her hand in the kitchen sink, she noticed a splinter of wood in it too. Using her index finger and thumb, she took the wood chip out of her skin and tossed it on the floor, red droplets staining the linoleum. Actual, real, honest-to-God linoleum, not that vinyl crap. Her eyes caught sight of the stray mushroom from last night, sitting there under the table, begging for attention. She decided to ignore it.

"Brendon! Come on, we're going to be late!" Sheree called as she dried off her hands with a dishtowel. The cuts seemed to have clotted quickly she noticed as she took the towel away to inspect the wounds, for they had stopped bleeding and were now just a little pink around the punctured areas.

As if on cue, Brendon ran down the steps, jumping over the broken posts, and flew out the doorway screaming out his goodbye to his parents as he did so. Sheree also said bye before walking out, closing the door behind her. After she opened the door to her little blue sedan, she unlocked the passenger's side for Brendon from the driver's seat. Hurriedly, he opened the door and slid into the car. Fastening her seatbelt, Sheree put the car in DRIVE and did a U-turn toward the main road. Storybook Lane was the next street over, but there wasn't a cross-street from Song's End, so she had to drive to Main Street and take two rights to get to Brendon's school. Ravenwood Elementary was actually built right over the grounds of the original one-room schoolhouse that once stood alone on the barren road. It had just started raining when Sheree turned into the parking lot.

SCREECH!

The car slid out of control as she put her foot on the brakes, spinning around and moving in the opposite direction. Sheree tried to gain control of the steering wheel, but it wouldn't budge.

"Oh noooooooo!" Sheree shrieked, still trying desperately to regain some form of control of her vehicle.

"Watch out!" Brendon cried, clutching his seat with both hands as he saw where the car was heading.

Sheree shifted the clutch into NEUTRAL and slowly lifted the parking brake, hoping that would work. It was a strategy she had seen in a video that was shown in the driver's education class she took earlier that summer in Seattle before they moved. Within seconds, the car came to a stop. *Thank God I remembered something from that course,* she thought to herself.

"That was a close one," Brendon said with a relieved expression, letting out the breath he was holding onto and releasing his hands from the seat. The small indentations in the cushion slowly puffed back to shape. He also checked his crotch area to make sure he hadn't involuntarily pissed his pants, letting out another sigh of relief that he hadn't.

Lifting her head up, Sheree saw that she was only inches away from a large maple tree, only one of many that lined the north side of Storybook Lane. Without much thought, she quickly reversed back into the road, dropping Brendon off before heading to Ravenwood High, though she seriously considered ditching school since the universe obviously had it out for her that day, and it had barely begun!

The drizzle had died down and the sun was breaking through the deep gray and black clouds. The bright light blinded Sheree as she turned south on Main Street. *Great,* she thought, shielding her eyes with her left hand. *The one day the sun decides to come out, I forget my sunglasses at home.*

Chapter 3
More Spiders, More Voices, More...

"C'mon Sheree, do you really think that Chad likes me?" Jennifer Hoang, Sheree's newfound friend asked with engrossed enthusiasm.

"Yes I'm sure," Sheree answered. "He couldn't stop talking about you in biology."

Jennifer tossed her straight black hair away from her face and smiled. Her parents had come to America from Vietnam only a few months before she was born. Once a year, usually during spring break, they made a trip back to Vietnam to visit relatives still living there. Her dad wasn't home very often, one business trip after another keeping him away, leaving the house with just her mom and herself.

Sheree took another bite of the greasy cheeseburger she had gotten from the lunch counter then dropped it onto the tray. There was only enough for about one bite left, but for some reason or another, that piece was the part of the sandwich that had all the fat and calories, so if Sheree were to eat it she'd get fat. Or so she told herself. After she drank what was left of her chocolate milk, she crushed the paper carton in her hand, some of the foam at the bottom of the container oozing out of the opening and onto her fingers. "Mmm, chocolaty bubble goodness," she said as she licked her fingers.

"That's the best part," Jennifer told her.

"I'll be back in a minute Jen. I'm going to throw my garbage away. Want me to take anything while I'm up?" she asked, standing up from the bench.

A nod from Jennifer indicated that she didn't have anything to be thrown out just yet, so Sheree walked over to the can and peered in. Blinking a few times, she hoped that she was only imagining what she saw. It didn't work. Thousands of small, dark, black things were crawling around. They were spiders. Thousands upon thousands of small, black, spiders, inching their way over the inside of the aluminum trash can. Her tray was tilted into the bin and one of the spiders took advantage of this, climbing onto the tray and then onto Sheree's arm.

"Aaaah!" Sheree screamed, dropping the tray into the garbage.

The cafeteria suddenly became quiet, everybody looking in her direction to see why she had screamed. Jennifer ran over to Sheree, wondering why too. *I wish these people would stop staring, she thought as she sprinted toward her friend.*

"Spiders!" Sheree shrieked frantically, her eyes full of fear. "Don't you see them? There are hundreds of them, thousands of spiders! Help me! Help get them off of me! Please!"

"Sheree! Calm down, there aren't any spiders!" Jennifer assured her friend, holding onto her thrashing arms to keep them from harming both herself and Sheree. "I don't see anything, there's nothing here."

First looking into the garbage can and then at her arms, Sheree saw that the spiders were gone. They had disappeared. Embarrassed, she ran out of the school cafeteria and into the hall, tears streaking down her face. Jennifer ran after her, chasing her into the girl's restroom to see what she could do.

"Are you okay?" Jennifer asked, opening the stall Sheree had plunged herself into, poised upon the toilet without an ass-gasket for protection.

"I saw spiders, real spiders, crawling all over me. I swear. I mean, I must be the only one who could see them. Or maybe that is their master plan, to make everyone think I'm crazy and then I'll be popular for all the wrong reasons because I'm all cuckoo for Coco Puffs or something. Well it's not going to work, not now, not ever. I will be popular because I'm cool, not because I'm a nutcase!" Sheree screamed, the sound echoing off the walls.

"Oh my gawd, you're on drugs aren't you? Wait a minute, you're on drugs and you didn't ask me? What kind of friend are you?!" Jennifer inquired accusingly.

Letting out a laugh of relief, Sheree told her friend, "I'm not on drugs, and if I was, you know I'd share with you."

With a shake of her head, Jennifer snapped back, "Okay, so maybe you aren't on drugs, but if you were you'd want to take me down with you? Oh my gawd, I can't believe I actually thought you were cool!"

"Jennifer!" Sheree screamed, horrified that she'd offended her best friend.

"I'm just joking. Geez, chill girl. But to tell you the truth, something made you react the way you did to the inside of the garbage can, and I can tell you right now what it is."

"Really? It was spiders, wasn't it?"

"No Sheree. It wasn't spiders. There were no spiders. If there were, I would have seen them because my vision is beyond perfect thanks to medical science."

"Laser surgery?"

"Yep."

"Great, so I really am crazy. Okay Jen, make the call. It's time they take me away wearing a straight jacket and lock me up in one of those padded rooms. The Oaxaciian Tribe Mental Health Center is only a mile away, right?"

"Yeah, um, that's not going to happen. Besides, it's crazy that they named that loony bin the Oaxaciian Tribe anyway, because there are no living Oaxaciians left. I mean, the entire tribe was wiped out except for Chief Ravenwood."

"Really?" Sheree asked, "They're all dead?"

"And there's more. You know that street you live on, well, let me tell you all about it…

"Song's End was the seventh son of Chief Ravenwood, leader of the Oaxaciian (Oh-ah-ha-kee-en) people. His father named him Song's End because he was born at the end of a tribal ceremony, the sacred song having just ended when Ravenwood's wife gave birth. Many of the Oaxaciian people were frightened of the newborn. The child had been born with teeth, two of them, pointy canines, and many knew that the prophecy was coming true.

"Ancient traditions and legends of the Oaxaciian told of an evil that would threaten their existence, who would be born the seventh son of the chief of their tribe. Ravenwood assured his people that the gods would not choose to take them away, that the prophecy spoke of another seventh son, not his own. However, Ravenwood should not have been so ignorant.

"The legend gave specific instructions on how to eradicate such an epidemic from happening. According to the prophecy, the child must not be allowed to feed from his mother's breast, or she will die. The child must be immediately wrapped in his father's cloak then taken to an area far from the tribe, buried under seven stones, and left there for seven days. After the sun has set on the seventh day, the stones are to be removed and the child's wrapped corpse burned.

"Ravenwood, certain that his child was not the evil the prophecy spoke of, allowed his son to live, despite much opposition by the tribal council. The council had tried to persuade their leader that taking such a chance was not wise, but Chief Ravenwood would not hear of it. His newborn son was to be raised and taught the traditions, as all other children in the tribe were. However, it was not much longer before Ravenwood himself began doubting his decision.

"Song's End was only a few weeks old when he got his first taste of blood. Nursing from his mother's breast, he dug his teeth in and began sucking the blood. His mother tried to pull her baby off, but he was too powerful, and she quickly became weak from the blood loss. She screamed out, hoping someone would hear her in time, but when the handmaidens and Chief Ravenwood arrived it was too late. Song's End had drained his mother's life force completely.

"Ravenwood, grieved over the loss of his wife, admitted his failure to believe in the prophecy and prayed that the gods would return his wife to him. It never happened. The tribal council begged Ravenwood to kill the child immediately, before their entire civilization was destroyed. Chief Ravenwood finally agreed that it had to be done. Ravenwood took Song's End to a remote area of the surrounding forest and proceeded to wrap his child in his cloak. Still angry for the child taking his wife, he decided not to wait the seven days under the seven stones, and instead built a fire and watched the body burn.

"Upon returning to the tribe, the council greeted Ravenwood. They all informed him that after the seven days of being buried under the seven stones, they would all be witnesses to Song's End's burning. Ravenwood then informed the council that would not be necessary because he had already burned the body and made sure there was nothing but ashes.

"The council became frightened and called Ravenwood foolish, and told him that he was responsible for the inevitable genocide that will sweep over the tribe in the coming years. They told Ravenwood that because the ritual was not performed correctly, that he had inadvertently made Song's End immortal, now more powerful in death than he ever would have been in life.

"Ravenwood tried to assure his people that because the child was wrapped in his cloak, that his soul could not escape the fire and was destroyed along with his body. However, not long after the death of Song's End, one by one the children began disappearing. Great search parties were sent into the woods to find the children, however they never returned. The women of the tribe began having tormenting nightmares and started having extreme sexual desires, then becoming weak and losing their strength. The men too became sick and weak. All of the children had vanished from the tribe and the men and women, sick and weak, were the only remaining people left. Chief Ravenwood and the council, also experiencing the same plague as the rest of the Oaxaciian people, prayed and sacrificed to their gods, forgiving them for the loss of their children and hoping that they would cure the disease they were all stricken with.

"It was not long before the women began dying, their blood drained from punctures through the neck. After the women were all dead, the men began dying off too, murdered by draining the blood, but with the men, large gaping holes were found in their necks, as if having been bitten by a wild animal. Ravenwood was soon the only surviving member of the tribe, and although he died of natural causes many years later, he had gone crazy and completely delusional. Nobody had ever mentioned seeing who or what it was that was killing off the people, but everybody, including Ravenwood, knew that it was Song's End."

"Well, that story right there answers your query. The Oaxaciian people were clearly all crazy themselves! Maybe they found some wacky tobacky in the forest or something, smoked it, got the munchies and started eating each other because they were so out of it!" Sheree stated, beaming one of her beautiful smiles. "Mmm, doesn't quite taste like chicken, but dude, it'll do."

Quickly covering her mouth and making an odd expression, Jennifer said, "Oh my gawd, you just said 'dude'! That is so retro!"

"Dude, I did. Oh my gawd, what is wrong with me?!" Sheree shouted. "Slap me next time I say that! I mean, I'm such a dork."

"Ew, I just looked dork up in the dictionary, and you'll never believe what it means," Jennifer said with a look of disgust.

"What?" Sheree wondered, suddenly curious as to its definition. "I always thought it meant a stupid person."

"Yeah, but it also means penis."

"Oh, now that's just gross," she told her friend. Feeling better, Sheree sat up from the toilet seat, checking out her butt to make sure nothing was stuck to it. "See anything?"

Giving a quick look, "Your ass looks great, Sheree. I wish my ass looked like that," Jennifer informed her.

"Turn around, Jen," Sheree commanded and Jennifer obliged. "Now c'mon, your ass is way cuter than mine."

"Shuh, I don't think so. Mine's all small and ten-year-old-boyish, and yours is like, 'hello, may I direct your attention this way please!'." Jennifer shook her head and put her right hand on that side of her face as she looked down at her Hello Kitty watch. "We really should get to class. We're already ten minutes late."

A look of dread swept over Sheree. "Why don't we just skip the rest of our classes? I've had one helluva bad day and I need some release. Wanna go shoe shopping?"

Jennifer's eyes lit up. "Love to!"

Peaking out of the restroom door, they made sure the coast was clear before running to the student parking lot. Charlie, the creepy school security guard rent-a-cop guy who's always hitting on the hot girls, was too busy smoking a cigarette to notice them as they hopped into Sheree's little blue sedan. As they pulled onto Main Street from the school, they both shouted, "Payless, here we come!"

Driving down the road toward the Ravenwood Factory Outlet Shopping Center, Sheree turned to Jennifer and asked, "Wait a minute, you said you knew what it was that I saw in the garbage can, so what was it?"

"No, I said I knew why you had that reaction," Jennifer corrected her.

"Minor difference, what was it?"

"Your chocolaty bubble goodness, of course! That chocolate milk is made with cocoa processed with Energizer batteries!"

"Okay, there's no way that 'alkali' and 'alkaline' are the same thing. I mean, why would they make chocolate milk using essence of Duracell?"

"It is. I looked that up in the dictionary too."

"That's gross. I mean, grosser than the dork-penis gross."

"Yeah, let's just focus on happy thoughts, okay?"

"New shoes, new shoes, new shoes," Sheree repeated as she drove into the outlet center's parking lot.

Looking at each other, they both shouted again, "Payless, here we come!"

"The itsy bitsy spider went up the water spout…"

Sheree instantly woke up when she heard the familiar sound of the small child singing the lullaby. Carefully she lifted herself off her bed and walked over to the floor vent.

"If that's Brendon, he's going to get it," she told herself, her hands balled into fists and her face all scrunched up and a sneer on her mouth.

Carefully tiptoeing across the room and over to the door, she put her hand on the knob. As slowly as she could, she turned it and pulled the door open just enough for her to get through.

CREAK!

Sheree cringed.

The singing continued.

She quickly walked over to her brother's room right across the hall and opened the door, hoping to catch him in the act. But there she saw Brendon sleeping in his bed, holding his dirty yellow blanket that he'd had since he was a baby in a position that looked like he was making sweet-sweet love to it.

Fear ran through her entire body.

It became hard for her to breathe.

The air began to get heavy.

Heavier by the second.

Heavier.

Goosebumps started crawling over her skin, the hair on the back of her neck standing on end. She became cold and shivered, hugging herself. The air continued to get heavier and heavier and she kept getting colder and colder. Her eyes widened with terror.

She rushed back to her room as fast as she could, slamming the door behind her. Searching for the light switch in the dark, she fingered her way to the plate and flipped it up, but the light didn't turn on. She flipped it up and down several times, but the light would not work.

Singing continued.

The air getting heavier and heavier, harder and harder to breathe.

Her body getting colder and colder.

Sheree's eyes were fixed on the vent.

There was a blue-green light gently pushing through it, almost mist-like.

Quickly, she jumped onto her bed and pulled the covers over her body.

The singing wouldn't stop, it just kept getting louder and louder and louder.

Shivers ran through her back, the blankets on her bed that she was hiding inside were not enough to make her warm up.

The air was still heavy.

The singing still getting louder.

The strange light getting brighter.

Still cold… cold with fear.

Shutting her eyes, she hoped it would all go away.

Silence.

She opened her eyes.

It was morning.

Was it all a dream? she asked herself, slowly lowering the covers.

Getting out of her bed, she walked over to the door, creak after creak following her. Putting her hand on the doorknob, she began to turn it, but stopped after glancing over to her light switch. It was sticking up, but the light wasn't on.

It brought her back to the night before when she was furiously trying to turn the light on but it wouldn't shine. She walked over to the center of the room and looked up at the light bulbs in the ceiling. Standing up on her bed and carefully examining them, she noticed that they were burnt out, all three of them. Staring up at the painted white metal light fixtures, she saw a faint blue-green tint gleam onto them. Turning around quickly and facing the vent, she again saw the light coming out of it.

All the fear came back.

The cold, the heavy air, everything.

Her eyes again filled with terror.

"Why is this happening to me?!"

Sheree's eyes were glued to the light that was bursting through the air vent. The light was getting brighter and brighter, quickly illuminating the entire room. Terrified, she watched as the luminosity continued to get brighter and become a mist, filling the space. Suffocating her. The brilliant light was so intense it was the only thing that she could see, the rest of her room lost in the haze. As Sheree tried to pry herself from the radiance, the more it clutched onto her, like it was a force dragging her into its world, pulling her in against her will.

"Mooooooooom!"

Did I just scream? Sheree asked herself.

The light had made her lose her sense of mind and she felt like she was far off in the distance, away from everyone else. She was being taken over by this teal light hypnotically casting a spell upon her.

Brendon ran out of his room and jumped down the stairs, his expression of complete horror. "Mom! Dad!" he screamed as he ran, flailing his arms in the air.

Blinking a couple of times, Sheree realized that Brendon's last call had brought her out of the trance she was in.

Yes! He saw the strange light, too.

The mysterious light was gone, no trace of it ever having invaded her room. Without a thought as to how it had suddenly disappeared, Sheree ran down the steps to the kitchen. Brendon was seated on a stool while Mr. and Mrs. Hollins were intently listening to their son explain what he had just seen. As Sheree walked in on the conversation she saw her little brother's terrified little round face as he spoke.

"Sorry Brendon, the light's gone," she informed everyone, feeling a little disappointed.

"Huh? What on earth are you talking about?" Mrs. Hollins asked her daughter, completely perplexed.

Realizing that Brendon wasn't telling them about a strange light or creepy lullaby that had forced its way through the vent, she quickly came up with an explanation. "I'm sorry, I meant to say that my lights burnt out. Don't know why I was apologizing to Brendon." She smiled and half laughed it off, hoping they'd believe that was all she was up to.

"Oh," Mr. Hollins said with a grunt. "All three of them?"

"Yeah," Sheree told her father, shaking her head. "The weirdest thing."

"Well, I'll go change them in a minute then."

Curious as to why Brendon was screaming, she decided to ask. "What's all the hubbub about?"

"Brendon was just telling us that he saw hair under his armpits," Mr. Hollins told his daughter in a sarcastic tone.

Sheree rolled her eyes.

It's probably mold.

"Are you feeling okay, Sheree? You saw a blue-green light coming out of your air vent?" Jennifer asked with a concerned look on her face, about to put her hand on Sheree's forehead.

Knocking Jennifer's hand away, Sheree asked back, "You don't believe me either, do you?"

"Can you hold this a sec?" Jennifer requested of Sheree, handing her the strawberry ice cream cone they had gotten from a rolling cart vendor in the park so she could put her sleek jet-black hair in a ponytail. "Thanks." Jennifer smiled as she took the cone back.

"You didn't answer my question." Sheree seemed a little hurt, so she took another lick of her chocolate ice cream cone to make her feel a little better. She loved chocolate. It was one of the few things that could calm her down.

"Well, come on Sheree, it is a little hard to believe. I mean, would you honestly believe someone if they told you that they saw a green light coming out of their vent?" Jennifer asked her friend matter-of-factly, suddenly picturing said light coming out of a vagina, quickly adding, "Before your incident, of course."

Jennifer's dark eyes stared into Sheree's.

"I guess you're right Jen," Sheree said, smiling.

"Damn girl, what am I going to do with you? Spiders in the school cafeteria, and now this strange bluish-green glow seeping out of your bedroom's air vent." Shaking her head, Jennifer suddenly realized something. "Your eyes!"

"What?" a perplexed Sheree asked.

"Your eyes, they're blue-green. Maybe there is some phosphorescence in your air vent leftover from a broken fluorescent light bulb, and the house is old, so it is probably inadvertently emitting some form of radiation that is possibly causing a reaction between it and the phosphor. Just a theory," Jen said, trying to put a logical spin on the incident.

When did Jen get smart? Huh, must just be an Asian thing, Sheree thought to herself, buying into the stereotype. "Okay, but that doesn't explain the little kid singing."

"What?!" Jennifer shouted, nearly causing Sheree to lose grasp of her ice cream cone, which would have made her sad and possibly homicidal. "You heard singing too?"

"Yes?" Sheree question-answered warily, suddenly not sure she should have ever brought up the whole event.

Letting out a loud sigh, and taking another lick of her ice cream, Jennifer said, "Well, there must be some scientific reason for this, and…"

"Not everything can be answered by science!" Sheree yelled ferociously, her eyes wild and wide. Saturdays were not supposed to be filled with interrogations and scientific theories.

"Calm down now," Jennifer said, patting Sheree's thigh like a concerned grandmother. "I've got a theory on that too. Perhaps, and just bare with me on this one, there could be an old talking baby doll lodged somewhere inside your floor vent. And every time the forced air turns on the doll sings…"

"…that it's going to kill me? Yeah, nice theory, but I'll stick to my version. That house is haunted and someone doesn't want me there. It's as simple as that."

Without another argument about it, Jennifer simply said, "Okay," and left it at that.

Simultaneously, they got up from the park bench they were sitting on in Ravenwood Park, licking their ice cream cones while they walked around. They passed the ice cream vendor who took his time staring at their rear ends and nodding his head slightly with a grin plastered on his smooth and well-groomed college-boy face.

Sheree stared at the ground while she walked.

Jennifer began to feel a bit uncomfortable.

Great, she thinks that I've lost it! My best friend thinks that I'm crazy. Again!

Following a dirt path, they entered the dark, densely wooded forest where the trail winded. The entire town of Ravenwood was engulfed in the dense forest, the very reason the Oaxaciian tribe settled it, and years after their demise, Edmund William Blaire settled it. Back then it was known as Blaireville as he had named it after himself, but after his good friend Chief Ravenwood died, E.W. Blaire renamed the town to honor him.

"Hey, Sheree," Jennifer started to say, trying to bring up a conversation to lighten the mood before continuing in a sing-song voice, "I heard that Jeff Mains has the hots for you."

Sheree looked up and beamed a great big wide-eyed toothless smile. "Do you really think so?" she asked, crinkling her nose.

"Are you kidding?! He's hot for your bod! He's warm for your form! He's…"

"I got the point!" Sheree shouted, her face blushing from embarrassment.

"He wants to drizzle fo' shizzle on yo' nizzle!"

"Stop!"

It made Jennifer happy to see a smile on Sheree's face that wasn't forced. Strolling along the path, they continued to talk to each other, Sheree asking Jennifer if Chad had gotten the courage to ask her out yet. Much to Jennifer's dismay, he hadn't.

They walked deeper and deeper into the forest.

The farther they went, the darker it got.

Darker.

Darker.

It was so dark that neither of the girls could see the path any longer even though it was only mid-afternoon. A cold, spine-chilling wind rustled through the vast trees. The freezing wind whistled as it swiftly blew between the leaves and needles and branches, getting louder and louder.

It sounded like screaming.

Children's screaming.

Endless screaming.

Their sight weakening as it grew almost pitch black.

Unbearably dark.

Suddenly a bright greenish light blinded their eyes as it flashed toward them.

"The light!" Sheree screamed in horror, every muscle in her body freezing.

Flashing in every direction, it cast eerie shadows over the forest floor. And what sounded like laughter was bouncing off the trees. Evil laughter, like that of a villain or a madman, filled with malice and loathing, despising everything good and innocent and pure. The green light dimmed as their eyes became used to its brightness, but the laughter seemed to be getting louder and closer and even seemed to be multiplying.

"Oh my gawd, is that what I think it is?" Jennifer whispered, in shock that her friend's experience might in fact be true.

Sheree couldn't speak. She was too afraid; too afraid to even move.

Suddenly the light began changing colors, from the green to a blinding white then to a bone-chilling blood red. Over and over the light switched, like a cheesy 1950s B-movie special effect for a UFO.

"Cool! This is the neatest flashlight!" they heard.

Both Jennifer and Sheree looked to the base of the illumination and found a child playing with a Playskool flashlight, surrounded by four or five other enthralled kids gawking at his toy.

Figures, Sheree told herself, knowing that it was too good to be true. Knowing that Jennifer must still think she was crazy. Knowing that she had to prove to Jennifer that what she'd heard and seen in her bedroom was real and not just a figment of her imagination, a horribly abhorrent hallucination.

"Well that's a relief!" Jennifer said loudly, a chuckle following.

"Yeah, what a relief it is to know that I'm just nuts!" Sheree said back. "Just call me 'Crazy Annie'!"

"Who?" Jennifer asked, confused as to the reference.

Shaking her hand and closing her eyes, Sheree answered, "Sorry, just some homeless woman we used to make fun of back in Seattle."

"That is just sick, making fun of less fortunate people." Jennifer was clearly disgusted by this admission.

"No!" Sheree shouted back excitedly, "that's not the worst of it. She used to wear these really small shirts, and she was by no means a small person, so her flabby belly would stick out as she carried her plastic bags down the street along Alki Beach, wobbling from one side to the other like a Weeble. Some people used to call her 'Belly' because of that!"

"Eeeauuw! Everyone knows you need a figure like ours to pull off a belly shirt! God invented pretty people for a reason, and that is to show off their tummies," Jennifer informed Sheree, pointing to her own well-toned and naturally tanned stomach.

Still in disbelief over what her best friend just said, Sheree shot back, "Wow, you're not conceited."

"I call it honesty. It's just the truth, you know, and people have got to live with it whether they like it or not. And if they don't like it, they can kiss my tiny little waist!"

"Or your tiny little barely-there ass!"

"I hate you," Jennifer scowled.

Sheree scowled too, imitating her friend. "We should go back to the park where there is some light. This place gives me the creeps." *Why would I go into a forest ever again after…*

"Yeah, the forest is just crawling with spiders, and I know how they make you feel." *Even the imaginary ones.* "We should go," Jennifer agreed. "Oh, and speaking of spiders, I've got another theory on the cafeteria incident too."

"Oh gawd Jennifer, not another one of your theories?" Sheree said in doubt of her friend's conjectures and their relativity to her situations.

"No, really, just hear me out. You were probably just reliving the spiders you saw crawling around in your cereal. Just a flashback," Jennifer told her.

"Hmm," Sheree thought, "you might be right on that. But I don't remember telling you about finding spiders in my cereal?"

Jennifer looked stunned. "You must have told me. How else would I know?"

"You're right," Sheree told her, waving her hand down like she was swiping away the last comment she had made. "Unless of course, you were the one who put spiders in my cereal?"

"Last I heard Spider-Os are a nutritious part of a balanced breakfast. They have the wholesome goodness of Cheerios with that wonderful arachnid crunch people just *die* for!" Jennifer said in a commercial quality voice with the goofiest smile upon her slightly tilted face.

Laughing, Sheree said back, "You're a nerd, really."

"Just don't call me a dork," Jennifer told her. "I just had ice cream and projectile vomit runs in my family."

"Thanks for the good advice."

Walking back to the park, Jennifer said, "Just between you and me, that flashlight scared the crap out of me. Literally. Do I have anything showing? What a day to wear white shorts! It's just like the day I started my period all over again."

Chapter 4
The Basement

"The itsy bitsy spider went up the waterspout…"

Sheree woke up instantly and turned on the lamp on the nightstand expecting it to blind her for a second, but not expecting the intensity of light coming out of it. Her dad insisted on having the highest watt bulbs available on the market for all the lights in the house, even though their energy use would cause the electricity bill to be outrageous. When her mother suggested the new compact fluorescent bulbs instead to cut down on energy costs, he freaked out about how unnatural the concept was and told her he didn't want to hear another word on the subject, especially given how "damned expensive those swirly things are." she remembered her father saying. As Sheree's eyes adjusted, she looked at the bulb mount of the lamp and noticed it had written on it to not use any bulbs higher than 40 watts, and she knew that it had a 150-watt bulb screwed into it.

Well that's not a fire waiting to happen!

"Jennifer, wake up. The voice, it's singing again," she told her friend, glad that she convinced her to stay over, especially since it was Labor Day Weekend and most families in the Northwest make camping plans. Moist, soggy, damp camping plans because that is what you are supposed to do in Washington State. Oregon, too.

Still groggy, Jennifer sat up and rubbed the sleep out of her eyes. She had to shield them from the brightness the lamp radiated. "Sweet Baby Jesus, is that you Buddha? Have I died and this is the light to heaven?"

"It's just my lamp," Sheree assured her friend, rolling her eyes.

Unable to see still, Jennifer turned her head away. "What were you saying?"

"The voice from the vent, can you hear it?" Sheree asked, praying for a response in the affirmative.

Putting her ear to the vent, Jennifer listened for the voice Sheree had spoke of. "Oh, wow. I can hear it."

Sheree felt relieved. She was beginning to think that maybe the noise was just a part of her imagination because no one else in the house could hear the singing that came from the vent. Of course, that didn't explain her other supposed hallucinations about spiders and blinding teal light. Now that Jennifer could hear it too, she knew that it was real. Smiling, even though she was terrified and delighted at the same time, she turned to Jennifer, noticing her face was expressionless as she listened to the twisted lullaby.

"Let's go down into the basement. Maybe the person doing this is down there," Jennifer suggested, pulling her head away from the vent, waiting for Sheree to answer.

But Sheree hesitated.

The basement? "Are you crazy?" Sheree asked her friend, trying to figure out if she was serious or not.

"Come on," Jennifer said as she grabbed Sheree's hand and walked out the bedroom door into the hallway, guided solely by the lamplight.

"Oh my gawd, you are serious, aren't you?" Sheree said while she was dragged down the steps, the creaks seeming so loud in the quiet house, each one making her more and more uneasy. She could not help but stare at the slight bend in the middle of the rail and the three missing posts beneath, hoping her father would fix it soon because with her track record, she'd find a way to fall through the void. Then again, she'd land on the living room sofa… if she was lucky. At the moment, however, she wasn't feeling very lucky.

They had reached the door to the basement and stood in front of it. Jennifer put her hand around the doorknob and turned it slowly. The antique knob squealed as it was rotated. Frightened, Sheree looked at Jennifer and gave her an I-hope-you-know-what-you're-doing look as the door opened. A gust of musty air greeted them, gently breezing through.

Sheree's heart began to pound.

Faster and faster.

Louder.

"Where's the light switch?" Jennifer asked while she looked around the dark murky room.

"Beat's me," Sheree answered with a slight shrug. "I've been in here once and I didn't like the feeling I got."

They both looked around with curiosity. Sheree decided that it wasn't that bad when her best friend was at her side. The basement didn't seem as scary as it had her first time in it. Of course, the door was still open.

A long silvery strand caught Jennifer's eyes. "I think I found it," she said, tugging on the metal-beaded string. An immensely bright light flooded the entrance stairs. "Man! Do all the lights in this house have five hundred watt light bulbs?!" Jennifer joked, shielding her eyes from the unexpected blast that immediately began toasting her raised arm.

"Actually I think they're six hundred," Sheree joked back.

They giggled as they carefully walked down the aged steps. Sheree swore she could feel the boards bow like a trampoline as she walked on them. Endless steps that didn't seem to lead to anywhere, they just kept going on and on, farther and farther away from the safety of the rest of the house. Surprisingly, despite the immense flood the light bore at the top, it began to fade as they went deeper into the basement, as if the dark was consuming the light.

Deeper.

Finally the flight of stairs ended and they were on the basement floor.

"Let's split up," Jennifer told Sheree, noticing that the basement was as large as the rest of the house. Or what she could see of it anyway.

"Are you effing kidding?!" Sheree shrieked, eyes wide, not believing the words coming out of her friend's mouth. "We should stick together. I'm just too scared."

"You're right. I don't know what I was thinking," Jennifer agreed, brushing her hair behind her ear.

Cobwebs filled the cellar.

They walked around, looking at everything; the boxes of winter clothes that would soon need to be taken up; the plastic Christmas tree with all the ornaments and lights still on it; an old painting of one of Sheree's long dead relatives that scared the shit out of her when her eyes caught sight of it.

I feel like I'm walking on a conveyer belt, Sheree said to herself.

Treading across the floor, Sheree felt her legs tingle. She had expected the concrete floor to be cold as ice, but it was surprisingly warm. The tingling sensation continued, slowly moving from her socks and up her bare legs. Deciding to brush it off, she figured it was just her mind playing tricks on her, and continued to search for a clue. Something that would produce a brilliant blue-green light or something or someone that was singing the lullaby, but she wasn't finding anything except the family's old junk.

An itch had formed on one of her prickling legs, and had it been winter she would have assumed it would be because she hadn't shaved them, but being summer they went through the daily torture of razor blades, so she reached her hand down and started to scratch it. Then her hand began itching. Then her arm. Whatever it was had spread all over her body. Scratching her arms and legs furiously, trying to make the tingling go away. She scratched and scratched but it wouldn't stop.

Her body began to get warm and sweaty.

The tingling and the itching getting harsher and harsher the more she scratched to relieve it. She scratched her arms and her legs and her back harder and faster, her nails digging into her skin, tearing it from her body.

Jennifer.

Where was Jennifer?

Sheree couldn't see her anywhere.

She had disappeared.

Vanished.

Irritated and burning with pain, she bent down to scratch her feet. Her hand touched them, but they seemed to be buried. It was as if they were buried under thousands of smooth clumps, softer than rocks, harder than dirt.

What is going on? Am I sinking?

Trying to lift her hand out of the clumps, she realized that it was being pulled in. Tugging harder and harder, she gave it all she had to free her hand until it finally was liberated of the strange peculiar nuggets.

Curiosity getting the best of her, she lifted her hand to the light emanating from the top of the stairs to find out what was covering her feet. Terror filled her eyes, widening wider and wider until they could not any longer. She tried to scream, to tell someone, but nothing could come out of her mouth, not even a squeal.

Her face turned pale with fright, the blood draining out.

Her heart pounded with incredible strength.

Faster and faster.

Louder and louder.

Then she couldn't breathe. She tried to, but she couldn't.

Gasping for air, but it wouldn't enter her mouth.

Wanting to rid her hand, her body of the things that were all over her, she tried to move, but she couldn't. She was frozen in place. Like the forest. Like the cafeteria.

Turning her eyes back to the stairway, she saw Jennifer's silhouette, watching with her arms crossed and staring right back at her. She just stood there, watching as Sheree was in horror. A grin extended across her barely defined face.

Sheree felt like she was sinking down into the ground.

Her feet were covered above her ankles.

Fear ran through her now numb body.

Then the light went out.

The darkness reigned.

Sheer blackness.

Standing motionless in the gloomy basement, Sheree could feel the presence of evil surround her.

Watching her.

Preying on her.

Hot and sweaty, a drop fell from her forehead.

Footsteps walked closer and closer to her.

Closer.

"Jennifer?"

Nothing.

"Is that you Jennifer?" Sheree asked again, hoping to get a response as she felt the thousands upon thousands of small insects crawling all over her body, pulling her, burying her alive. The pitter-patter of their thread-like limbs moving across her bare arms and legs felt like blunt knives, stabbing her over and over as they walked every bare speck of skin.

"I'm here, Sheree."

Furiously pounding with abundant speed and force, Sheree felt as if her heart would burst right out of her chest.

Still sweating.

Still terrified.

Still dark.

"Don't be afraid Sheree," Jennifer said quietly. "Don't be afraid."

Jennifer sounded so distant, yet Sheree could feel her presence. How near she was, watching her as she was in horror.

The bugs continued to pace over her body.

She was still sweating, making her red, irritated skin burn with more pain.

"Don't be afraid," Jennifer repeated.

There was a long pause.

Silence.

So quiet that Sheree could hear the footsteps of the insects scrambling over her flesh; gliding down her wet back; returning down to her legs then climbing back up again as if her body was simply an amusement park ride to them.

"Don't worry... I'll take care of you."

What does Jennifer mean by 'I'll take care of you'?

Sheree heard Jennifer come closer and closer to her, seeming to take hours for what should have only taken seconds. But she still couldn't see anything, her eyes refusing to adjust to the black and suddenly wishing that she actually liked carrots because they might have improved her night vision.

The sound of bugs being crushed filled Sheree's ears.

The crunching getting louder the closer Jennifer approached.

Closer.

Louder.

"Goodbye Sheree."

A sharp pain ran through her head then throughout her body.

Sheree woke up, frightened and soaked from perspiration. She was sitting up with her arms holding her from behind. Slowly her eyes faded from the starry blackness to the light of day. Looking around, she realized that she was in an unfamiliar room, in an unrecognizable bed that seemed quite small for her. Her head ached with pain, especially the back of it. Machines surrounded her, connected to her, and making faint beeping and buzzing noises.

Mrs. Hollins walked through the door, her head bowed and her eyes tired. The copper hair that was normally so neat and styled looked disheveled and natty. It looked like she hadn't slept in days.

"Mom? Why am I here?" Sheree asked, trying to figure out what happened that merited a hospital and life monitoring computers.

Lifting her gloomy face, Mrs. Hollins saw her daughter staring back at her. "Sheree! You're awake!" She ran over to Sheree and hugged her like she had been away for a long time.

"Frank! Frank!" Mrs. Hollins called with excitement in her voice.

"What is it Beth?" her dad asked as he walked into the room, wearing scrubs and his photo name badge. Looking at the metal-framed bed, he saw Sheree searching around the room in confusion. "You woke up!" Her dad rushed to her side and gave her a long passionate hug and kissed her on the forehead. He smelled of formaldehyde and death.

"Can someone please tell me what is going on?" Sheree asked, still confused. "Ooh, my head." Lifting her hand to her forehead, she began rubbing it to make the headache go away, but realized the pain was coming from the backside and, slowly reaching around, felt a large lump. Instantly followed by another shot of pain, she removed her hand from the back of her head and put it back on her temple, rubbing again.

Mrs. Hollins took her daughter's free hand in hers and looked into her eyes. "You were attacked by a burglar. The doctor said that we were lucky to find you early enough or you might not have made it."

Slipping her hand out from under her mother's, Sheree put it on her head with the other one, trying to concentrate, to remember. But she couldn't recall being attacked by a stranger. Her hands slipped into her hair, disappearing into the golden strands, then reappearing out the top of her head.

"You've been in a coma for nearly a week," her father told her, sitting next to her on the bed. "We almost gave up any hope you'd pull out of this."

"A week!" Sheree shrieked, regretting it afterwards when her headache began pulsing even more, causing her to close her eyes until it receded. "What kind of parents are you? Don't you know you're supposed to lose hope after years and years of me being in a coma, but a week?" she said quieter, more upset that her parents had about as much patience as she did. "I swear, if I could, I would divorce you and go buy better parents."

"Same old Sheree," her father said, looking at his wife.

"Yes, apparently this little mishap didn't inadvertently lobotomize her, leaving behind a more agreeable daughter," her mother told her husband.

Rolling her eyes in disbelief, Sheree told her parents, "Don't you know anything? You lobotomize in the front of the brain!"

As they were all laughing, the door swung open and Jennifer entered the room, a card and a small vase of flowers in her hands.

"Sheree... you're alive!"

As soon as Sheree saw Jennifer, her eyes widened.

Her heart pounded with increasing speed.

Fear ran through her body.

She was back in the basement.

With the bugs.

Alone... with Jennifer.

"Get her away!" Sheree screamed, shielding her face and closing her eyes as if it would protect her. "Get her away from me!"

Looking at her friend in amazement, Jennifer was shocked that Sheree didn't want to see her; that her reaction was of terror. "It's just me, Jennifer," she assured Sheree, lowering her hand to Sheree's shoulder.

But Sheree knocked it away. "Go away you killer!"

Backing away and completely astounded, Jennifer almost tripped over Mr. Hollins.

"Sheree! It's Jennifer!" her mom tried to tell her. "She's been worried sick about you. Everyday after school she's come by to see how you were doing."

Confusion swept over Sheree.

Jennifer was the one who was down in the basement with me. She knocked me over the head, right? Why would she be here everyday to see how I was doing? Sheree asked herself. *So no one would suspect her, that's why. I've got theories, too.*

Cautiously, Jennifer walked closer to the bed, setting the flowers and card on a table that was filled with others just like them, still trying to figure out what was going on in Sheree's head that would cause her to freak out.

After calming down, Sheree saw a bandage on Jennifer's forehead and stared at it a second before looking into Jennifer's eyes with a questioning face.

"I also got knocked out by the maniac," Jennifer said with a grin, touching the bandaged wound with her hand.

She's lying! She's lying and she knows it!

Angry enough to strangle somebody, Sheree decided to keep it inside, hoping it didn't show on the out. Hoping no one would see her fury, her frustration.

"C'mon Frank, let's go tell the doctor that she's awake," Mrs. Hollins told her husband, grabbing his arm and exiting the room.

"You're mom and dad are so weird."

"Huh?" Sheree asked, not knowing if she heard right.

Suddenly realizing that she was thinking out loud, Jennifer told Sheree it was nothing. "I've got to get home soon so I can study, Sheree. Mr. Simonds is giving us a quiz tomorrow."

"Ugh," Sheree responded.

"I can't believe you're awake! It's amazing, the doctors said you'd have some brain damage and may not fully remember anything. But I see that you are still my paranoid little freak!" Jennifer told her, lightening the mood.

"Thanks for the reassurance, Jen," Sheree said, cracking a smile. *Hey Sheree, it can't be Jennifer. She's your friend.*

"Glad to see that you're okay," Jennifer said while squeezing Sheree's hand before strolling out of the room. The door immediately opened again and Jennifer reappeared, this time very serious. "Don't tell anyone about our little secret, or something bad might happen."

A chill ran down Sheree's spine as she liftwwed the covers to her face and slid under them to comfort her. Had she heard right? Was Jennifer really the one who tried to kill Sheree? She decided not to think about it. Just pushed it to the far end of her mind where she shoved all of her bad feelings and thoughts, where she kept them bottled up in a place so crammed full at the moment that it might shatter, causing a flood of emotions to rampage out of her like a herd of wild buffalo.

Chapter 5
The Plumber Dies

"I'm so glad to be out of that hospital and back into my own room!" Sheree said as she hugged her blue teddy bear that she'd had since she was six. It used to play "Lullaby, Lullaby" but years have passed since it last chimed the soothing tune. After throwing herself on the bed, she gazed at the ceiling, watching the sunlight play across the glitter embedded into the paint, dancing like tiny fairies against a sky of fluffy white clouds.

Ugh, I've probably got a ton of homework to do, she thought as reality set in.

So glad to be home.

So happy.

"The itsy bitsy spider went up the waterspout…"

Still gazing at the ceiling, the air got heavy and thick.

No, this is not happening!

The air got heavier and heavier, harder to breathe in the breath to live.

She started taking in short, rapid breaths, trying to suck in what she could.

Slowly, relenting to her fear, her eyes turned to the vent in the floor where the small voice again came gently rolling through.

Brendon walked in. "Sheree, wash up for…" but his words were caught short. He heard the voice singing. Looking at his sister, he saw that her fright-filled eyes were glued to the vent.

"And the itsy bitsy spider was out to kill again!"

Brendon jumped back as the last part of the evil lullaby was sung.

"What was that?!" he asked, almost not believing what he just heard.

Quickly, Sheree turned around, wondering when Brendon had entered her room. "You heard it?"

"Yes I heard it!" Brendon shrieked with a look of shock on his face, pointing, "It was coming out of the vent!" He gave his sister a look like he wanted an answer, but didn't really expect one from her. "Mom!"

Hearing the frightened voice of her son, Mrs. Hollins rushed up the stairs to see what Brendon wanted this time, hoping it wasn't more armpit "hair." Again.

Did Jennifer really mean what she said? Sheree wondered.

Mrs. Hollins walked into the room and Sheree put her hand around her little brother's mouth to prevent him from saying anything.

"What is it?" she asked with a tomato-stained wooden spoon in her right hand, dripping blood-red sauce onto the floor, indicating that it was probably spaghetti night and the much-dreaded mushroom would be playing a starring role at dinner.

"Oh, nothing," Sheree lied, plastering a smile on her mouth.

Rolling her eyes and wondering why she even bothered, Mrs. Hollins said, "Well it's time to eat, so wash your hands and get downstairs."

After their mother left the room and was at a safe distance out of earshot, Sheree let go of her brother. "Don't tell anyone, okay?"

Looking at her like she was crazy, Brendon said, "We have to tell someone."

"Brendon, please?"

"Whatever." He shrugged his shoulders and rolled his eyes and left her room.

Breathing a sigh of relief, Sheree went into the bathroom and turned on the faucet. Nothing came out, so she tapped the top of it, thinking it might have a clog or possibly even a small rock, something she found was common with their old water well. Still nothing. Becoming frustrated, she put her head under the spout to see if she could find what was causing the faucet not to work. Unable to see anything blocking the water's path, she moved her head out from under it.

"Hmmm," she thought, wondering what she could do.

Suddenly a thick, red liquid started gushing out.

It looked just like… blood.

Quickly, she closed her eyes as the warm, heavy liquid poured out of the aged faucet, thick and red.

"Fresh blood," Sheree said with a pleased smile as she sniffed the perfumed air, opening her eyes to admire the site of blood splashing over the sink and onto the counter. The beauty of the red covering the avocado sink reminded her of Christmas, was more than she could handle, and practically had to resist lowering her face in to lap the blood up with her tongue. But she couldn't. As if entranced, she plunged her face under the faucet, gulping down the warm liquid flowing out of the tap, savoring every salty-sweet drink, some trickling from her lips and over her chin, down her neck. After having her fill, she wiped her mouth with her bare arm, smearing it across her face. A look of complete satisfaction was over her.

"The plumber must have finally died."

Pulling open the cabinets under the sink, she peered in. The plumber was there. His eyes wide open and his face filled with horror, a pipe wedged into his slightly hairy bare chest. It was just barely possible to see the 'Billy' on his navy blue shirt right above the company logo 'Plumb and Get It!', a small amount of blood having leaked out, covering most of the badge.

So pale.

So frightful.

So… dead.

Sheree's eyes opened and she saw the ceiling, sparkling with the glitter she painted when the family moved in a little over a month ago.

How long had she been asleep?

Brendon walked into her room and told her to wash up for dinner.

Damn. I knew it was too good to be true, Sheree thought to herself, sitting up in her bed and glancing over to the vent. "What the hell, Sheree!" she said aloud. *You actually wanted the bit about drinking plumber blood to be true?*

The room slowly faded to black and she felt weak as she stood. To steady herself, she leaned her hand on her bed until the room faded back into view, gently rubbing her fingers over the stitching on the quilt she used as a bedspread, a quilt her great-grandmother made her when she was a child and was threadbare in spots from having been washed so many times and in desperate need of repair, but she couldn't bear the thought of not having it near her, covering her, protecting her.

Why do I feel so weak? she wondered, walking out of her room to the bathroom to wash her hands. *Oh yeah, I just got out of a coma.* The light was on when she entered it. *When will Brendon ever learn to turn off the light after he leaves a room?* Shaking her head at her last thought, she reached for the faucet. Suddenly her dream flashed back into her mind, unable to escape the vivid images that were like snapshots being thrown at her face.

The blood.

The plumber.

With her hand grasping the handle of the faucet, she pulled it up. To her relief only water gently flowed out of the spout. The sound began filling the room, getting louder and louder. She was about to put her hands in the warm water when out of the corner of her eye a small dark figure crawled out of the drain.

"Eeeuuw!" Sheree shrieked in disgust, her face twisting.

Looking at the creature reminded her of the corrupt lullaby that had been haunting her, especially the last line. Without much thought, she grabbed a square of toilet paper and positioned it in her hand. Eyeing the creature's every move, trying to capture the sordid thing. Her fingers squeezed hard as she caught the spider, crushing it inside of the tissue; greenish yellow goo that had bled through moistening her fingertips. Lifting the lid of the toilet, she tossed the wrapped spider's carcass in and flushed it, making sure that it had completely vanished from her sight before closing the lid.

The gushing water from the faucet sounded again after the toilet finished refilling the bowl. Quickly, she thrust her hands into the water to clean them of any of the viscid substance that had leaked through the paper. After she was certain that her hands were sanitary, she splashed some water onto her face. When she finished, she pushed the faucet's handle down and reached for a towel to dry off. The towel felt so soft, like a comforting blanket. She held it to her face for a few extra seconds after she was dry just to feel the softness of the hand towel and smell the fresh scent of the fabric softener. It felt so good she didn't want to take it off her face, but slowly she managed. Her eyes widened and she stopped breathing while she watched in horror as an arm limply fell out of the cabinet.

Hysterical laughter burst from the under-sink cabinet.

Is that someone laughing or is it just my imagination? Sheree wondered.

The cabinet door flew open and Sheree's eyes enlarged, her head shaking slightly, her breathing becoming more like a shorted pump desperately gasping for air.

"Noooo!"

The laughing continued to get louder, and colder, and ruthless.

Brendon's body plopped out of the cabinet with a loud thud!

She stared at her lifeless brother.

When did the laughing stop?

Bending down, she turned him over onto his back. Her hand quickly covered her mouth in disbelief as she looked into his face.

"Gotcha!"

"What? You little creep!" Sheree yelled, falling back and catching herself on the wall.

Brendon couldn't help but laugh. His sister looked so scared, more so then he had ever seen her. Even more than when there were spiders in her cereal and when he locked her in the basement.

"You are evil," she said to him, standing up from the olive linoleum floor.

A small grin ran across her face as she trotted down the steps, hardly able to believe that she thought Brendon was dead. Noticing the missing posts still hadn't been replaced, she wondered if her father was actually going to fix it or if her mother would get tired of seeing the hole and do it herself.

Much to her dismay, it was indeed spaghetti night. And yes, there were mushrooms. As she sat down in her usual chair, her foot caught hold of something, and to her disgust, it was the mushroom she dropped on the floor a couple weeks ago. Instead of picking up, she left it there, curious to see how long it would take for someone else to notice the slimy, rotting fungus on the hardwood.

Chapter 6
You Are Evil

Things were going really well for Sheree the following week. It appeared that her new relationship with Jeff Mains was spelling L - O - N - G - T - E - R - M , something Sheree never thought would happen since her previous boyfriends only lasted a few days. Most of them just thought she was another dumb blond, and when she would get intellectual, they would freak out. Perhaps they thought because she was so much older than most of the other students in her class, she must be stupid. Of course, so few people knew about the tragic circumstances that surrounded her delay into school, as well as subsequently being held back a grade, that most people just assumed her IQ was below average.

Jeff asked Sheree out the day she got back to school. They had an instant connection. By lunch they were holding hands. By the time the last bell rang, they were already making out. And surprising even herself, they went on their first date that night. A school night! And her parents said it was okay!

"Sorry, Sheree, I can't seem to stop staring at your eyes," Jeff told her, holding her hand across the table while they waited for their pizza at Ravenwood Bar & Grill, a local hot spot for touring bands, craft beers for those old enough to drink it, and the most amazing pizza.

Sheree blushed, another surprise as she was usually known to taunt girls for getting all goo-goo over a boy. But this wasn't any boy, this was Jeff Mains; master of soccer, king of compliments, the student every teacher dreams about. Jeff Mains, who helps the special education kids get to class. Jeff Mains, who volunteers to help elementary children learn to read. Jeff Mains: Genuine, Honest, Caring. Sheree could envision the billboards saying that last part when he runs for mayor after college, not even certain if he had those ambitions. He was with her, holding her hand, and nothing else mattered.

But that was last week, and there were a week's worth of dates with Jeff that progressed to even more amazing levels of bliss Sheree never thought possible. However, things between Sheree and Jennifer were getting colder than ever. It wasn't the fact that Jeff and her started dating that drove them apart, since Chad was now in her life thanks to a random happenstance involving Jennifer and the male cheerleader practically saving her life from a projectile pom-pom aimed at her head, albeit, as a friend since he was too chicken-shit to ask her out. It was the uneasy feeling Sheree had that Jennifer was involved in the attack that caused her to be in a coma for six days.

Thoughts like that can ruin a friendship.

"Aargh!" Sheree growled as she slammed the cordless phone down on the charging unit.

"You and Jennifer fighting again?" Mrs. Hollins asked politely, not bothering to look up from her home magazine she was reading in the living room.

"Rolling her eyes, Sheree screamed, "Uh, duh!"

Peeling her eyes from her article on How to Deal with Ungrateful Teenagers, Mrs. Hollins (laughing on the inside at the irony of the situation) asked in the same polite tone as before, "About what this time? Boys? Sex? Your bangs? Her bangs? She bangs, she bangs! Oh baby yeah she… sorry. Ricky moment there."

Unable to be angry any more after watching her mother put moves to the lyrics of the new Ricky Martin song, Sheree burst into a sputterful laughter. So sputtered, it was almost lathered in spittle. "Thanks, I needed that, Mom. Really hectic week."

"Really? Having that much trouble getting back into school after, well, you know, the coma?" her mother asked with worry, hoping nothing was seriously damaged in her daughter's brain from the trauma.

"No, it's not that. It's just that it seems Jen is either completely pissed at me or she's my best friend. I mean, since Jeff and I have been going out, it seems she's been jealous of the time I'm spending with him and not her." Sheree sighed, oblivious to the fact that she was spending an inordinate amount of time with her new boyfriend compared to everything else. "Do you think it's possible for your best friend to be your worst enemy?"

Her mother rolled her eyes at the illogicality of Sheree's question. "No, but it is possible that your enemy could be your best friend," she offered.

"Same difference," Sheree said, shaking her head ever so slightly.

"No, different but the same," Mrs. Hollins corrected, as if implying a distinction between the two.

"Okay, help me out here, Mom. I'm blond."

"I'll make it simple."

"Yes. Please. Use small words and enunciate. Blond," Sheree informed her mother, pointing out her hair color.

"Would you still be friends if she blatantly stabbed you in the back?" Mrs. Hollins asked her daughter, hoping that the word 'blatantly' wasn't too big of a word for her until she remembered it was Brendon who probably wouldn't know it.

"Literally or figuratively?"

"Either. Take your pick."

"Well, no."

"See. But would you still be friends with someone who all fingers point to, but there isn't any hard evidence, just coincidence?" After saying this, Mrs. Hollins mind wandered. *Is 'coincidence' the right word? Or is it 'coincidents' or 'co-incidents'? Maybe 'coincidences'?* Before she could finish her thought, Sheree interrupted by answering the question she had just posed.

"Yeah I guess, 'til I could prove otherwise."

"Now do you see my point?"

"Oh my gawd, you had a point?" Sheree asked, wide eyed. "Just kidding, it makes sense now. Just sounds better the other way around."

"Story time!" her mother announced in a Sunday School Teacher-like voice, full of phony excitement, patting the space on the couch next to her to motion Sheree to sit.

"Huh?" a dumbfounded Sheree uttered.

"It's story time. This is the part where I tell you a little bit about my life and how it relates to yours. Very interesting, you won't want to miss it," Mrs. Hollins informed her, still using the annoyingly fake tone, still patting the adjacent couch cushion.

Raising her hands over her closed eyes and plopping onto the sofa, Sheree said, "Fine, just drop that voice."

"Yeah, okay. Well, you know how tumultuous your relationship with Jennifer is? My roommate and I in college were like that. We were practically inseparable. Then I met this guy and people started talking about how he had apparently cheated on me with my best friend, but I wouldn't believe it, even when Suzy Barton, who I swore had been born on this earth to torment me since I entered kindergarten and seemed to follow me around just to make my life hell, told me she saw them making out at a party. But I figured that she was lying and everyone else was just making crap up because he was always in our dorm room with me. I mean, we spent more time there than his place because his Frat Brothers would always be hanging around, and, well, we needed some privacy!"

"Over Share!" Sheree yelled, covering her ears.

"Sorry, anyway, as it turned out, Suzy was right. My roommate was just a backstabbing bitch who seduced my boyfriend by telling him she'd do things that I would never do, which was just not true because I'd already done a lot of those things and so many more and I really have no idea where she would have gotten the idea that I was some sort of prude or something."

"MAJOR OVER SHARE ALERT!!!" Sheree shouted at the top of her lungs, her eyes now so wide it wouldn't surprise anyone if they just fell out of their sockets and landed in her lap before self-destructing.

"You're sixteen now, I think you are old enough to deal with the fact that your mother was a slut," Mrs. Hollins said matter-of-factly to her increasingly squeamish daughter.

"MOSA! MOSA!"

"I mean, your dad and I even carried on a three-way for almost a year when you were a toddler."

"MOSA! MOSA! MOSA!"

"Fine, so I moved out of that dorm room and it just so happened that Suzy had just lost her roommate, so I moved in with her."

"Your sworn enemy?!" Sheree screamed, throwing her hands in the air at the absurdity of it all.

"Yes, because she was up front and honest about it. It got me thinking that maybe it was me who was being unfair to Suzy. After all these years, she wasn't trying to piss me off, she was just honest, and I always took it personally. And we have been best friends ever since."

"You mean Suzy Arroyo? What ever happened to your boyfriend? Did you totally humiliate him in front of all his little frat buddies?" Sheree wondered.

"Worse, I married him."

Sheree's eyes lit up. "You mean you were married before Dad?"

"No you dumbbell. He is your dad! I really don't know how you can be such a great student, Honor Roll and Advanced classes and still not have a clue about the obvious."

"But he was cheating on you with your best friend!"

"Well it's not like I wasn't cheating on him with his best friend Bobby!"

"Arroyo?" Sheree screamed, standing up and pacing. "You people are sick. Gawd, and here I was thinking about what a bitch Jen has been since we got whacked over the head by some psycho nut job, and my own parents are completely abnormal! You know that right? Your behavior is straight out of a bad daytime soap opera."

"I guess I shouldn't tell you that my old roommate is your Aunt Beki then, should I?" her mother asked with a not-so-innocent twist.

"Oh, that's just sick! She's Dad's sister! That is wrong on so many levels, I just don't know how to begin to count them!" Sheree said, raising her voice and finding her way toward a chair.

"Well, only technically. Beki was adopted by your grandparents when she was seventeen, and at the time, she was your dad's girlfriend, so that kind of put a damper on their relationship until they moved out and went to college," Mrs. Hollins told her, hoping to clear at least that one thing up.

"This is not happening, this is not happening," Sheree repeated over and over, rocking back and forth in the seat while hugging her core.

"Fine, I'll stop talking," her mother offered.

"Thank you. Thank you for me never again to be able to think of Aunt Beki as my favorite aunt, but as a dirty girl doing dirty things to my dirty dad! And thank you for giving me this horrible vision of you and Uncle Bobby getting it on in the boy's locker room."

"We only did it there one time!"

"You did not have to tell me that!"

"I know, I know, over share. So, to get back on topic, do you really think Jen is suddenly your worst enemy?" her mother asked, seriously.

Shaking her head, Sheree answered back, "I don't know. Maybe she is just jealous that I have a boyfriend and she doesn't. Maybe I should hook her up with Chad. Obviously the pom-pom I threw at her eye and he caught before it hit her didn't work."

"Chad Walker?" Mrs. Hollins asked, shocked and suddenly looking guilty like she got caught.

"Yeah," Sheree affirmed cautiously, brushing aside her mother's facial expression as an anomaly.

"I thought you said he was gay?"

"Yeah."

"So what makes you think that he'd be interested in a hot little Asian girl?"

"Hey, I don't want anybody violating my Jen! I'd rather set her up with someone I know will be safe."

"So she's your best friend again?"

"Both… at the moment. Or at least until I can prove anything. I mean, she seems to be the most common factor to all the crap that has been happening in my life."

Looking a little confused at the last comment her daughter made, Mrs. Hollins asked, "Like what?" hoping it wasn't anything serious.

Suddenly Jennifer's threatening words from the hospital flashed into Sheree's mind. "Oh nothing, just talking out my ass, you know me." Turning around, she grabbed her butt cheeks and pulled them apart in sync while she said, "Blah blah blah!"

"Okay, that's an over share moment!" her mother said, falling back in her seat and laughing heartily.

With her ass still front and center to her mother's face, she looked over her shoulder and said with a smile, "Hey, at least I didn't fart!"

And with that talk, Sheree took her mother's advice to heart, deciding that her friendship with Jennifer deserved a fair trial (and a watchful eye!) Besides, setting Jennifer up with a boyfriend would obviously allow her to spend more time with Jeff without having to argue with her.

After the second week with Jeff, Sheree had nearly forgotten all about the blue-green light and mischievous singing coming from her bedroom vent. Not only that, but now she and Jeff were the hottest couple at Ravenwood High, boosting her popularity level. It was, however, becoming increasingly difficult for her to keep her hands off of him, and she dreaded the time they'd spend apart while he volunteered so she started volunteering with him after school at the library Tuesday and Thursday. She wasn't sure what kind of power he had over her, but when they were together, she didn't care.

"Wow Sheree, things are getting serious between you and Jeff, aren't they?" Jennifer asked delightfully, quickly catching her friend before the weekend.

"Yeah, I can't believe it! He's just so great. I don't deserve him," Sheree told Jennifer as they strolled across the student parking lot. "Need a lift?"

"Nah, Chad's walking me home," Jennifer said, beaming a big grin. "He's so cute, and always wants to talk. Boys just aren't like that around here. They're usually all, 'like football, want to play?' and Chad, well, he's interested in a lot of the same things I am, you know?"

Chuckling, Sheree said, "So in other words, he's gay."

"Probably. I mean, he is a cheerleader, right? That'd be my luck, wouldn't it?" Jennifer asked without expecting an answer. "You have a great weekend. Call me!" she yelled as she ran over to her boyfriend and gave him a big hug before they walked away holding hands.

Even when Sheree first told Jennifer about Chad telling her that he had a crush on Jennifer, Sheree thought he wasn't quite straight, and almost didn't tell Jennifer anything at all. But, she just assumed that maybe he was like her cousin Frank (not her father Frank) who proclaimed he was an effeminate heterosexual. Of course, her cousin Frank was just weird all around, reading books like *Hitchhikers Guide to the Galaxy* and listening to

They Might be Giants CDs and dressing up like Judy Garland to do impressions of her.

"Hey sweetie," Jeff said, swinging from behind and wrapping his arms around Sheree's waist.

Craning her neck around, Sheree gave her boyfriend a kiss on the lips, reaching up to his head to stroke his soft brown hair.

"Hi honey. Have any plans tonight?"

"Well, I was thinking of taking my girlfriend out to dinner and maybe a movie afterwards," Jeff told Sheree, who had now turned around to face him and his beautiful blue eyes.

"Oh, that sounds like fun," Sheree said back to him, smiling.

Letting out a heavy sigh, Jeff continued, "But she can't make it, so you wanna come with me instead?"

Punching Jeff's upper arm with her right fist, she barked, "You brat! I could punch you! Oh wait, I just did. Well, I could punch you again!"

"Please don't," Jeff cried, rubbing his sore arm. "This is probably going to bruise as it is."

"Pussy," Sheree shot back.

"Wow, I know to never cross you. You're harsh," Jeff said, still rubbing his arm and holding back tears from the pain.

"I have a nine-year-old brother; this is not even touching the tip of the iceberg when it comes to my wrath. Trust me," a serious looking Sheree informed her boyfriend.

"You are evil," Jeff told her.

A cold autumn wind came out of nowhere, giving Sheree the shivers. "Brrr, I wasn't expecting that."

Taking off his black, purple, and silver letterman's jacket, Jeff said, "Here, put this on."

Pushing it back to him, Sheree said back, "My car's only twenty feet away, I'll be fine."

But Jeff refused, and proceeded to put his jacket on Sheree. "I'll get it tonight when I pick you up at six, okay?"

"Okay," Sheree agreed, pulling the collar up over her neck and noticing it smelled like Obsession by Calvin Klein, which almost made her climax in the middle of the school parking lot. "I'll see you then."

He leaned over and gave her a quick kiss before they parted. "I'm so lucky," Sheree said to herself as she walked to her car, putting her hands in the pockets of her boyfriend's jacket. As she drove home, she tried to figure out what she was going to wear for their fifth date, debating between two new outfits she had recently purchased from Old Navy. Ultimately she decided on a rust, chocolate, caramel, and cream sweater with matching scarf and a pair of khakis. However, she was going to spend the next three hours after she got home trying on every shoe she had, some of them four or five times, to find out which went best with her outfit. "I knew I should have gotten new shoes when I bought this. I don't have anything that works with it!" Sheree said to herself, checking every angle in her full body mirror to find out if the current pair of shoes went well enough to wear out in public.

While putting on a pair she had tried on earlier, she heard the doorbell ring. "Crap," she growled, zipping up the faux-fur lined boots she had just put on.

Her mother was walking over to the door to answer it when Sheree came flying down the staircase, barely touching the steps. "Ooh, I like those boots. They go great with the sweater," Mrs. Hollins told her daughter.

"Well that figures, they were the first pair I put on," Sheree said to her mom, reaching for the knob to open the door.

A gust of wind rushed through as Sheree opened the door. A few leaves from the old maple tree in the front yard found their way into the house as well.

"It's a bit chilly outside, you might want to bring a coat," Jeff advised. "I'd have worn mine but you took it."

"You punk!" Sheree screamed, getting ready to punch his arm again.

"Please don't!" Jeff screamed back, taking a step in the reverse. "My biceps are all purple from the pounding you gave them earlier."

Feeling bad, Sheree said, "Come on in. I left your letterman upstairs in my room." Welcoming the warmth, Jeff wiped his shoes on the doormat and stepped inside, Sheree closing the door behind him. "I'll be right back with it."

As Sheree was busy retrieving Jeff's jacket, her mother began inquiring about the plans for the evening. "So, after dinner at Maxi's Diner, you'll be going to what movie?"

"Some new sci-fi flick, I forget the name of it. But it looks really good," Jeff told Mrs. Hollins, glad that Mr. Hollins wasn't home yet otherwise the questions would probably be a lot more severe.

Just then, the front door opened. "Who's here?" Mr. Hollins asked, but his question was answered when he saw Jeff. "Ah. Hello young man. Taking Sheree out again?"

When she heard her father come in, Sheree quickly ran down the stairs, hoping to rescue Jeff before it was too late. "Hi Dad, bye Dad, bye Mom, gotta go, love you!" she said, grabbing Jeff and heading out the door before her parents had a chance to stop them. "Here's your jacket, let's go, quickly."

"No argument there!" Jeff said, putting on his letterman's jacket. "That was a great rescue. My hero!"

"You're welcome," Sheree said back, kissing his luscious lips. "Mmm, cherry!"

"I thought you'd like that," Jeff said to her with a smile, referring to the Chapstick he was wearing. "I also thought you'd like this too." Reaching into his pants pocket, he pulled out a gold necklace.

"Oh my gawd, it's beautiful," Sheree told him, noticing the locket dangling from the gold strand. She opened it up to find a small picture of them taken on their first date by a fellow student learning to use his camera for photography class and asked to take their picture.

"Turn around and pull up your hair, I'll put it on," he commanded and she obeyed, still in shock at receiving such a lavish gift so early in their relationship. After clasping the necklace, Sheree turned back around to face him. "It looks perfect on you."

"Thank you, I love it," Sheree said to Jeff, holding the locket again before putting her arms around his neck to kiss him again.

After their embrace, Jeff opened the passenger door for Sheree and let her into his car, quickly running around to the other side to get into it himself. As they drove off, Sheree's parents pulled back the curtains to the window next to the front door. "I don't know about that boy," Mr. Hollins said to his wife.

"Oh, hush Frank, he's a really good kid. And did you see that necklace he gave her?" Mrs. Hollins asked her husband.

Shaking his head, Mr. Hollins replied, "Yes I did. I think this relationship of theirs is going too far too fast. Besides, he's a junior and she's just a freshman and…"

"…they're both sixteen, don't forget that. They are still the same age," Mrs. Hollins reminded her husband. "I've got a good feeling about him."

"They're both sixteen and that's what I'm worried about," Mr. Hollins said matter-of-factly.

Mrs. Hollins smiled and playfully shoved him before they settled down in the den to watch the news before the pizza delivery guy came with dinner.

Driving down Main Street, Jeff kept turning to look at Sheree who was fixated on her new locket. It was intricately detailed for its small size, and Sheree was envisioning the two-inch gnomes who must have carved it when they pulled into the Maxi's Diner parking lot.

"Oh, here already?" she asked, surprised at how quickly they had arrived.

With only a smile as his response, Jeff got out of the car and went around to the other side to open the door for his girlfriend, reaching for her hand to help her out of the vehicle. As they walked hand in hand up to the door, Sheree was about to open it when Jeff reached forward and got to it first.

He's such a gentleman.

Maxi's was unusually slow for a Friday night and they were able to get a table secluded from the other diners at the request of Jeff. After they were seated and ordered their drinks, Jeff just sat across from Sheree, staring into her shimmering aquamarine eyes, a grin plastered onto his face.

"What is going on with you?" Sheree asked. "With all the staring and the smiling and the lack of verbiage I'm getting a little nervous!"

Sighing, Jeff responded, "I was just thinking how lucky you are to be with a guy like me."

Taken aback, and not quite sure she heard him right, she yelled a little louder than intending to, "WHAT?!"

Looking around to see if anyone had noticed the outburst, and finding that people were too busy spilling ketchup on their shirts to hear anything but their own mouths chewing, Jeff told her, "I'm just kidding. I was thinking about how lucky I am to have met such a wonderful person like you. You're unlike any girl I've ever known. Most girlfriends I've had were just so superficial and fake and thought that just because I'm a jock that I'm dumb and I'd be an easy lay. But you, you're smart and beautiful and quirky all in one! And I find myself falling more and more in love with you every day."

Putting her hand to her mouth, tears began falling down her face.

"Oh my gawd, I'm sorry!" Jeff apologized with wide eyes. "I didn't mean to, oh no, I'm so…"

"No! These are happy tears, I swear! See," she said, pointing to her mouth. "I'm smiling."

Relieved, Jeff told her, "Oh thank God. For a second there I thought I had upset you. Here it is our two-week anniversary, the most important one in any relationship and I thought I'd done something wrong!"

What? He said two-week anniversary. Is that even a real anniversary?! Of course it is stupid. Oh crap, he got me the necklace, and maybe he thinks I've got a present for him and I don't and…

"Will you calm down in there," Jeff told her as if reading her mind.

"How did you know…?"

"Your eyes were darting from left to right about a hundred times. You only do that when you are mentally arguing with yourself." He smiled again, causing Sheree to melt all over once more.

"Did you really say that you were falling in love with me?" Sheree asked him.

"Sheree, I've been in love with you since the day we met," Jeff clarified, adding, "What I said was that my feelings for you just keep getting stronger and stronger."

"I can't believe it, this is, wow. I was just telling Jennifer today the same thing about you."

"Really? You're not just saying that are you?"

"No, it's true! I love you Jeff Mains! I love you so much it aches when you're not with me!" Sheree proclaimed, standing up, not worried about how cheesy her words sounded. This time her yelling was enough to grab the attention of some of the other diners in the restaurant, but she didn't notice nor care. As far as she was concerned there were only two people in that place, her and Jeff. She reached over and kissed him more passionately than she had ever kissed him before. Their tongues were busy swishing around in each other's mouths when the waitress came to the table.

"Sorry your drinks took so long you had to resort to sucking the spit out of each other," the waitress said, dropping their sodas in front of them.

Slightly embarrassed, they pulled away from their embrace.

"Are you ready to order yet, or do you need some more smooch time to think about it?" she asked jokingly.

"I think we're ready, right Sheree."

Sheree nodded her agreement.

After dinner and a sci-fi movie—about the impending apocalypse they'd be enduring soon, being almost the year 2000 and all—that she absolutely loved, which wasn't a far fetch since she loved almost every science fiction movie she'd ever seen, Jeff took Sheree home, walking her up to the front porch.

"I had a great time tonight," he told her, pulling her in closer to him.

"So did I," she concurred, allowing herself to be pulled in closer to him so they could kiss goodnight. "I love you."

"And I love you," he said just before leaning in for the kiss, after which he waited for Sheree to be safely inside her house before heading to his car. *I'm going to marry that girl,* he told himself as he looked at Sheree waving back at him from the living room window.

After he had driven away, Sheree said to herself, "I'm going to marry that boy." And with a bounce in her step, she headed upstairs to get ready for bed.

Sheree pulled Jeff's head toward her, returning his kiss. She loved the way his soft, dark brown hair felt in her hands as she gently brushed through it with her fingers. She wanted to continue kissing him, not wanting it to end. It was Monday night and Jeff had taken Sheree back home after they were done studying. Most of the night, however, was not spent studying, but making out of course. Considering the grade difference between them, her a freshman and him a junior, and that they didn't have any classes together, it was obvious they weren't going to get much studying accomplished.

Jeff pulled away slowly, his eyes opening shortly afterwards.

A little disappointed, Sheree opened her eyes too, noticing that the windows of Jeff's car were fogged. "I had a great ti…" she started, but stopped talking when she saw the pale face pressed against the window.

"I wonder what that tastes like!" she heard Brendon say, his bloated face plastered with a deranged smile.

"Oh that is it!" Sheree screamed.

After telling Jeff that she'd see him in school the next day, she rushed out of the car to chase down her pestering little brother.

"I love you!" Jeff yelled to her from the car.

"I love you too!" Sheree said back to him, turning around and smiling.

Interrupting they're lovey-dovey goodbye, Brendon shouted, "You'll never catch me!"

Knowing she had no choice but to pummel her brother using whatever blunt object she could find, Sheree ran after him towards the side yard. Realizing what bad shape she was in, her legs began to ache after only a short while. *Ugh, I've got to start working out again. Why am I not a cheerleader at Ravenwood High? Oh, that's right. They wouldn't even let me try out for the team, those skanky whores! Especially Courtney. That bitch thinks I'm trying to take everything away from her when I just want to be involved!* Where had Brendon gone? She looked in every direction to find him, to pay him back, to get revenge on him for everything.

Locking her in the basement.

Pretending to be dead.

Everything.

With her hands balled into fists, her nails began digging into her delicate palms. The teal in her eyes was quickly becoming a murderous shade of red. Fury and rage rampaged through her body like none she had ever experienced before, and for what? Interrupting a private moment with her boyfriend? Had the bottle she kept all of her bad feelings locked up in finally burst open, the glass shattering in every direction, and the emotions, free from their imprisonment, now able to escape through every pore in her body?

Where is that little shit? Sheree wondered, running around through the yard, looking for a clue that would lead her to him.

Nothing.

Not even a footprint in the soft, moist dirt or blades of turgid grass her father spent manicuring to perfection every second he was away from the television or bedroom. Her anger caused her to breathe heavily. That and the sprinting she was doing. A warm trickle slipped down both of her hands. Lifting them up, she saw that her nails had cut into her palms and blood was oozing out. Suddenly she heard a *crack!* immediately followed by a horrifying *thud!* Instantly, she turned around to see what it was.

Her brother lied on the ground, motionless.

"Ha ha, I'm not going to fall for this one you little jerk."

Looking at his chubby little body, she was thinking of taking advantage of the moment and socking him in the chest. Still staring at him, she was expecting some sort of movement, but there wasn't any. He didn't move, just lied on the ground with his face to the dirt. Sheree's heart pounded fast and loud, each heartbeat throbbing.

Still, he didn't move.

Cautiously she walked toward him, anticipating him to turn around and start laughing like a wild hyena as he had on so many occasions because that was what he did. It was like his calling sign, his modus operandi. The light from one of the windows in the house cast eerie shadows and she swore there were little black gnomes dancing around his body.

His body.

So still.

A small puddle of blood caught Sheree's eyes, growing larger and larger. Painting her father's perfect lawn red. Again, the color combination reminded her of Christmas.

"NOOOO!"

Running into her house screaming frantically, hoping her parents would hurry, hoping someone would come. Mr. and Mrs. Hollins dashed to the entryway where they found Sheree crying and screaming.

"What? What is it Sheree?" her mother asked.

"Brendon," Sheree said, catching her breath. "He's hurt! He's not moving!"

Her father told her to calm down. "Where is he?"

"On the side of the house," she told her dad then pushed her way out the door, her face displaying the shock of it all.

While Frank followed his daughter, Beth rushed to telephone an ambulance. After the call, she ran to the side of the house, tears streaking down her face as she was preparing herself to expect the worst.

"Oh my gawd!" Mrs. Hollins screamed when she saw her son lying on the ground surrounded by a puddle of blood.

"Calm down Beth! You have to calm down!" Frank kept saying to his wife.

"Brendon! Oh my gawd, Brendon!" she continued to say, falling to her knees, her hands on her face.

Red lights flashed down Song's End along with a symphony of sirens. The firemen had arrived first, immediately followed by an ambulance. White shirted men ran to the back of the ambulance to open it up as the E.M.T.s rushed to Brendon.

Two police cars pulled up to the house, followed by one more.

After checking his vitals, the white shirted men carefully lifted Brendon onto a faded blue stretcher and loaded it into the back of the ambulance. Both Frank and Beth were about to go in with them, but one of the E.M.T.s said that only one person could go inside with Brendon.

"You go ahead and go," Mr. Hollins told his wife. "Sheree and I will follow in the car and meet you there."

Without hesitation, Beth quickly went inside the white van and it sped off to the hospital downtown. The few police cars went ahead of it—probably the whole Ravenwood Police Department— clearing the way down the nearly empty street. As Frank ran to the family station wagon, Sheree started jogging toward the wagon too, when a cold hand grasped her shoulder.

Chapter 7
Accidents Happen

The hand was so cold.

Cold as death.

Cautiously, Sheree slowly turned her head back, frightened of who she might see behind her. "Oh!" she gasped.

"Hey, Sheree, what happened?" Jeff asked with a worried look on his face, his eyes staring right into hers.

"Brendon… he… he… he fell out of a tree," Sheree told her boyfriend with a cracked voice, looking down at the ground to avoid Jeff's eyes but clutching the locket he had given her. "It's all my fault."

"Huh?" Jeff seemed perplexed, curious as to how Sheree could have caused her brother's accident.

"If only I wouldn't have chased him, none of this would've ever happened," her eyes began to fill with sorrowful tears; the warm, salty liquid dripping down her cheeks, landing on her shoes and that damned perfect lawn.

Gently wiping away the tears from her face, Jeff put his arms around Sheree to give her a comforting hug. He hated to see her cry like this. The first time he'd seen her cry it was tears of joy, but this time was much different. He could see all the hurt and pain she felt inside and he wished he could magically make it all disappear. "It's not your fault. It was just an accident, all right?"

He kissed her.

I've got to get going, Sheree thought as she pulled away from the kiss. *I can't keep Dad waiting. He wants to know how Brendon's doing.* "I have to go," Sheree told her boyfriend, finally looking up at him. Giving him a look of thanks, she turned around and continued jogging to her dad's car.

"I'll meet you there!" Jeff shouted to Sheree, getting back into his own vehicle.

Acknowledging his last words, she waved a hand back as she opened the passenger door, buckling the seatbelt once she was seated. The white station wagon backed out of the driveway and onto the road, Jeff's sporty red coupe trailing behind them.

He's so sweet, Sheree thought, looking in the rearview mirror. *I'm so glad that we're together. I don't know what I'd do without him. Oh, how I wish I could kiss his tender lips right now, and feel the softness of his hair in my hands. Bad Sheree, bad, bad! How can I be thinking about Jeff when my brother could be dying?* Sheree scolded herself for being so selfish.

"Dad, do you think that..." her voiced trailed off. Looking at her father's face, she saw small teardrops sliding down his cheeks.

I've never seen him cry before in my entire life. Did he cry when he had to take me to the hospital?

The drive to the hospital was torturous. The waiting room was worse.

"He's going to be just fine," Doctor Homnick assured a frantic Mr. and Mrs. Hollins, who had been pacing back and forth for the better part of an hour while they waited to hear any news.

Sitting a few chairs down from where her parents were standing, Sheree sat with Jeff by her side, comforting her. It was almost as if she was lost in her own little world, just sitting there in the waiting room, rubbing the locket she was wearing that she had gotten just a few nights earlier.

The doctor put his clipboard down to his side and looked at Beth and Frank, smiling. "He broke his nose and fractured his left arm, but nothing too serious." He pushed his wire-rim glasses closer to his eyes. "Brendon just got the wind knocked out of him from the fall, causing his body to go unconscious. It was probably just a survival instinct kicking in, his body reacting to the traumatic experience. You're very lucky. If he would have been any farther up in that tree, I don't think… he might have… he might not have been able to handle it." A slight shake of his head made Frank wonder if he was lecturing himself for blurting out stuff before thinking through the consequences. Being the same doctor who also looked after Sheree, he noted, "I don't know if it's good luck or bad luck you've got on your side. Perhaps it is a little of both." He gave Sheree a smile, but she didn't seem to notice.

Beth looked up at Doctor Homnick, her eyes red and swollen from the tears she had been crying. "We've already lost one child. I don't think I could live if I lost another," her voice trembling slightly as she talked.

What other child? Sheree wondered, not quite certain what her mother was talking about. Then, as if something hit her over the head, she looked up in sudden realization. "Kayla…"

Her mind raced back to that awful summer…

"Hey, let's go play hide and seek," Kayla suggested.

Brushing her doll's hair, Sheree seemed quite content. "I don't want to," she said, putting down the purple comb she was using and picking up the white brush next to it.

Scowling, Kayla interrogated further, crossing her arms. "Why not?"

"Because," Sheree said back matter-of-factly, "I'm four now. I don't have to play hide and seek anymore." Suddenly changing her tone, she became all cheerful, and offered, "Why don't we have a tea party? We can invite all of our animal friends!"

Disinterested, Kayla decided not too. She never did like doing any of the things that normal little girls do. A good time to her was making a mud pie and jumping in it, getting the mud all over her clothes and causing her mother to have a fit. Kayla was quite the rambunctious little tomboy, preferring trucks to dolls. However, as much as she begged her parents for a truck or car or gun or transforming robotic aliens or anything little boys wanted, they would instead lavish her with dolls and tea party sets and make-believe princess dresses, all of which ended up becoming Sheree's. At least Kayla had an incredible imagination, something that came to be rather handy since she didn't care for most of her toys.

Intent on having her tea party with or without her sister, Sheree went inside the house then returned to the front yard carrying a stuffed teddy bear and sat it on the ground where she had set up her tea set, informing the babysitter, who was busy talking on the telephone, of her plans. She liked her idea of having a tea party with the stuffed animals. Walking in and out seven more times, she brought back with her a stuffed toy each time she returned. Her party was quickly becoming overcrowded. A couple of the guests had toppled over from gravity, so Sheree had to help them back up, especially if they were to enjoy her tea!

Running around the yard, Kayla pretended that she was an airplane. As she swooped in closer to Sheree, she knocked over one of the guests at the tea party. Frustrated, Sheree quickly set Mrs. Anderson upright. An angered expression formed on her small, round face. She poured a small amount of imaginary tea, which was really just water, into tiny pink cups and passed them around to her friends to enjoy.

Kayla screamed, "Rrrum, rrrrum!" as she flew across the yard, her arms outstretched, and head facing the ground. Staring at the bugs, she pretended that they were people below her. "Rrrrum, rrrrum!" she continued, following a butterfly that was soaring through the air with grace and beauty. The butterfly was her enemy, she thought, and she was bound on catching it and tearing its wings off.

"Would you care for more tea Mr. Pooh?" Sheree asked her teddy bear. "Thank you Sheree, I would," Mr. Pooh responded out of Sheree's mouth. "Mmm, that's yummy," Mr. Pooh informed Sheree out of her mouth. "Thank you, Mr. Pooh. It's my new recipe!" Sheree told him, giggling.

Still following the butterfly wherever it went, Kayla didn't even realize that she had trotted into the road.

HONK! HONK!

The horn caused Sheree to jump and turn around. The huge truck slammed on its brakes, but it was too late. It couldn't stop in time. Sheree began to cry as she watched her sister being crushed by the truck, blood soon filling the road as the beautiful blue butterfly fluttered out of sight.

"Kayla!"

Sheree blinked back to the present. "I'm sorry, what was that?"

"I asked if you were okay," Jeff repeated, gazing at her with his caring, concerned eyes, his hand rubbing her back.

"Yeah," she replied, pulling a clump of hair out of her eyes. "I was just thinking about my sister. I can't believe that I completely forgot about her."

"Oh." Jeff wasn't sure what to say, or even what he could do.

Looking up, Sheree noticed that Doctor Homnick had left and her parents had seated themselves a few seats from her. Quietly so as to not alarm her parents, she said, "I mean, she was my twin. How could I just forget all about her?"

Removing his hand from her back, he put his arm around his girlfriend's shoulder to bring her closer to him, and told her in the same quiet but less panicked tone, "There's no reason to beat your self up over it. How long ago did you lose her?"

"We were four. Oh my gawd, I can still hear the truck honking its horn!" Sheree cried, burying her face into Jeff's chest. Swooping her up with his other arm, he pulled her in even closer and began stroking her long hair, chanting, "it's all right, just let it all out," a few times, before finally she stopped crying and just sat there, letting herself be held and comforted, breathing in Obsession by Calvin Klein.

As Sheree was in Jeff's arms, she realized she had never before felt this comfortable with another person in her entire life, and never would have let a boy show this much affection to her in front of her parents. It was as if that stigma had been erased, like the moment you grasp the reality that this person is it, they are the one, and suddenly you don't care who knows about it. Without realizing it, a smile had managed to find itself on her face.

A tall, plain nurse walked over to them, her dark hair, which looked like it was starting to gray, was wrapped in a tight bun on the back of her head. "You can visit Brendon at anytime before eleven, but looking at my watch, it's already ten-forty-five, so you might want to go now." Her voice was low and about as simple as the rest of her.

"Thank you, Annie," her father said as he and his wife got up, adding, "You know, it's bad enough that I have to spend my days in this place, I'm kind of getting tired of spending my nights here too."

Shaking her head, Mrs. Hollins said, "Well, at least you work in the morgue where you only have to deal with dead people, and not hurt and whining and screaming people begging for attention because they have a hangnail or something horrible like that."

"True," he agreed (while Nurse Annie mumbled under her breath, "Lucky bastard.") "But still…"

They all looked over at Sheree still sitting down. However she motioned for them to go ahead, so they went to Brendon's room without her. Sheree noticed the nurse's walk was about as unremarkable as the rest of her. The vomit colored scrubs didn't help.

"Don't you want to go see your brother?" Jeff asked, brushing her golden hair out of her eyes.

Turning to face him and taking her legs off the seat and placing them onto the floor, Sheree said, "Yes, but I want to wait until my parents come back."

"Okay," he simply replied as he looked in her eyes, his face getting closer.

He's going to kiss me. Do I want him to? Yes.

His lips finally met with hers. The kiss was long and passionate. It helped Sheree get things off her mind, to relax. For a second, she pulled away gently to catch her breath, and then locked her lips on his again, kissing longer. Thoughts of her sister and brother were replaced by thoughts of how they had only been together for a short time and how she couldn't shake the feeling that this relationship was going to last as they continued to kiss.

If only she knew what would happen later that night.

After her parents returned only minutes later, she got up to go to her brother's hospital room at his request, hence the short parental visit. "I love you, Jeff," she told him as he prepared to leave, causing her father to cringe and her mother to put on one of her goofy smiles she usually reserved for cheesy romantic movies.

Smiling, he again told her, "I love you too," which caused her father to cringe even more, and her mother to put on a goofier smile that she usually set aside for cheesy romantic comedies. "I'll see you tomorrow."

Giving him a smile back, she decided to hell with it and rushed over to Jeff to kiss him before he left. Now to this, her father simply covered his face with his hands, shaking his head and mumbling nondescriptly, and her mother let out one of those laugh-cry noises middle-aged women going through menopause have a tendency of making. After letting go, her mom walked over to him as if she wanted a piece of the action too, but instead just gave him a hug and thanked him for coming. Sheree waited until he had left the waiting area before going to her brother's room. But before she had even gotten a few steps, she realized she didn't know where she was going. After asking her parents which room it was, she strolled down the monotonous hallways. Room 213, she saw on the door, the room she was looking for. The large, metal door opened smoothly as she pushed it even though it felt very heavy. Noticing that she only had a couple minutes before visiting hours were over according to her watch, she walked over to a chair and sat next to the bed where Brendon was lying.

"Hi Brendon," she said quietly, picking up his hand and gently squeezing it, not expecting him to look so horrible.

Opening his eyes, both of which were black and bruised, Brendon saw his sister's face above him. "Sheree," he said weakly, "I have to tell you something."

Leaning in closer, she asked, "What is it?"

"Tonight when I was on the tree branch," he tried to say, his voice dry, crackly, "I-I felt like I was… pushed." He tried to sit up straight, but gave up at his attempt as it was far too painful. "One minute I was holding onto it tightly, and the next I was flying toward the ground."

"It was probably just the wind or something," Sheree told Brendon with a heartfelt half-smile, hoping it would comfort him a little.

Shaking his head, he told her, "No. It couldn't have been the wind. It felt like hands on my back… shoving me."

"Why would someone push you out of a tree?" Sheree asked flat out. "And who else would be in our tree anyway? Think about it."

Brendon didn't give her an answer, he just looked forward at the faded blue hospital sheets as if he was contemplating her question and ignoring it at the same time.

Looking up at Brendon, her face serious, Sheree stated, "Unless I pushed you."

"What?" Brendon asked almost choking on his own saliva that finally decided to reactivate.

Leaning closer to him, Sheree lifted her arms, her hands reaching for his neck. "You heard what I said."

Her hands grasped hold of his neck, getting ready to strangle him.

Sheree grinned, a curious twinkle in her eyes. "Gotcha!"

"Oh my gawd!" Brendon yelled, regretting it right after as he recoiled from the pain. "You really had me going there. I was like, oh great, this is it, I've finally pulled too many pranks and now she's snapped!"

"Damn, so you were prepared and everything? I should have taken my chance while I still had it!"

"Ha ha, you think you're so funny, Miss Poopy Head."

Chuckling, Sheree said to her brother, "You know, we Hollins's have got an uncanny way of getting out of school, don't we?"

"Oh that's right!" Brendon shouted, not caring about the pain as it seemed numb by his joy at the moment. "I'm going to have to miss school thanks to this!"

After a few laughs, Sheree gave her brother a light hug and told him that she had to go before the hospital police come and take her away for staying in his room after visiting hours. Just as she closed the door, the tall plain nurse walked by, nodding approvingly with a slight smile. The nurse entered her brother's room to check up on him and find out if he needed anything. As she walked back to the waiting room, she was surprised to see Jeff standing there, talking to her parents.

"I thought you left," she said, still shocked.

Fidgeting, he said back to her, "I was going to, but then I decided not to."

As if a little hurt, she told him, "But we kissed in front of my parents and told each other 'I love you' and everything. How are we going to top that for a night?"

A perverse thought entered Jeff's mind, and Sheree was thinking the same thing.

"On second thought, don't answer that," she commanded, shaking her head.

They started talking, her parents by her side, discussing stupid, outdated hospital rules, and her mother was getting all worked up over the hours of visitation.

"It's just dumb," her mother proclaimed. "I don't understand the reasoning for it! I mean, he's just a baby."

"He's nine," her husband reminded her.

"A child nonetheless, and he needs his mommy." She growled. "Oh, Frank! There's Dr. Homnick, go get him, I need to have a word. Maybe you can pull some sort of rule-bending favor from him since you work here or something." Without hesitation, he rushed over to the doctor and led him over to his wife, who looked quite furious. "Yes, I have to talk to you about this visiting hours nonsense."

Before her mother had a chance to go all ape-shit on the good doctor's ass, Sheree said, "Jeff's going to take me home, all right? I've gotta get some sleep or I'm going to be a zombie in school tomorrow."

Beth turned toward her daughter. "You go ahead. We'll probably be a while talking to Doctor Homnick." She reached out and gave Sheree a hug. "Goodnight honey. Drive safe, okay Jeff?"

"Sure thing, Mrs. Hollins," he assured her.

Giving her father a hug too, Sheree told him goodnight and away toward the elevator they went. Not having the quietest voice at the moment, she could overhear her mother talking to Dr. Homnick about her dilemma.

"I just don't understand how you could impose these lame rules when there are children involved. I mean, he's only nine and…"

Cutting her off, Dr. Homnick told her in a hushed tone, "Nurse Myers is off in a couple minutes," and looking around to make sure nobody could hear him, he continued, "I can sneak you in after she's gone."

The last thing Sheree heard was her mother thanking the doctor as the elevator door closed. Knowing good and well that they could have taken the stairs down to the parking garage just under the main floor, she was glad they didn't. It may have only been two floors down, but she was afraid that with the luck Brendon and her seemed to be having lately, she'd fall down them and break her neck. On the plus side, if they did go down the stairs and she fell and broke her neck, at least she would have done it in the hospital!

Looking a little confused, Jeff tried to remember where he parked as they stepped out of the elevator. Suddenly the sporty little red coupe caught his attention and they treaded out through the parking garage toward it, passing columns and what few cars were in it at the late hour. After opening the passenger side door, he helped Sheree into the car, closing the door once she was situated in the seat. He did his mock-run to the driver's side he always seemed to do after letting her in, something Sheree didn't quite understand, but never asked him why he did either. Reaching around to the back seat, Sheree grabbed Jeff's letterman jacket and put it on. After putting his seatbelt on, he gave Sheree a quick smile as he put the key into the ignition, seeing that she was wearing his jacket again. He started the engine then made his way toward the road.

What a beautiful night. No clouds, a soft wind, bright stars and a glowing moon. It's the perfect night, Sheree thought, no longer worried about her brother, looking out the window. She turned and looked at Jeff, his eyes concentrating on the road, making a left turn onto Song's End. *And I'm spending it with the perfect man.*

The car stopped in front of her house and they sat in it, silently. Then Sheree seized Jeff's head and pulled it towards hers, their lips engaging in a kiss. The kiss becoming harder and more urgent than she had intended, but now that she had started, she couldn't stop, needing it to go on. Realizing that Jeff was trying to pull away, she pulled his head harder against her, forcing him to continue the kiss.

A few minutes later, Sheree finally let go. Noticing a peculiar taste on her tongue, she reached into her mouth and pulled out a piece of dull, mint flavored gum. "I believe this is yours," she said handing Jeff the sticky, green glob.

They giggled.

Their eyes met again.

"Do you want to come…?" Sheree started to say, but stopping herself once she realized what she was about to offer.

He looked right into Sheree's eyes.

Why is he just staring at me like that? Crap! He does want to come in! Well, at least my parents aren't home so we'll have the house to ourselves for a while. Crap! I've got a pile of dirty underwear on my bed. Crap! I didn't even make my bed! Crap!

But he didn't say a word.

Just stared.

A little freaked out at the silence, she looked at his gaze. It wasn't at her, but past her, behind her.

"Is there someone at your house?" Jeff asked, still staring.

"Huh," she said with a contorted face. Turning her head toward the direction that his stare was focused on, she now knew why. A faint yellow light was shining through the living room window, a silhouette slowly moving around. Someone was inside the house!

A stream of fear shot through her body. Who could be in her home? It couldn't be her parents because they were still at the hospital with Brendon. Was it a burglar, possibly the same one who knocked her and Jennifer out that night in the basement? Or maybe it was the person who pushed Brendon out of the tree earlier that night.

"I'm going to find out who's in there. You coming with me?" Sheree looked at Jeff for an answer before opening the car door.

With a little (okay a lot of) hesitation he told Sheree that he would go. They carefully walked through the front yard. Looking straight ahead, Sheree noticed that the only light on seemed to be the lamp next to the living room window, which wasn't at all unusual since they always left it on when they weren't home. However, as they approached the front door, they noticed that the figure they'd seen just seconds before was gone. Then suddenly Sheree looked up as she saw the light in her bedroom come on.

"Did you see that?" Sheree asked Jeff quietly, not removing her eyes from the window.

"See what?" His eyes gazed up to where hers were staring. "They must be in your room now."

"This is creepy."

They were standing at the front door, and Sheree was going over in her head whether or not to open it. Should she call the cops? Should she scream real loud? After mentally debating it for only a second, she reached out to open the door. It was locked. *Huh, why is the door locked? They must've gotten in from the back door.* Reaching into her jean pocket, she got her keys out and pushed the house key into the keyhole to unlock it. The door opened with a loud creak. "Great, now the whole neighborhood's probably awake," she told Jeff quietly.   Slowly they walked into the archaic house with caution, Sheree's eyes wide and searching with fear. Hoping that there was no one in the house; hoping that it was all a bad dream; wishing that it was over; knowing it was really happening. They tiptoed as quiet as they could over to the staircase, uncertain if the intruder had heard them open the front door. After taking one step up, she noticed that someone was looking down at her and Jeff from the top of the stairs.

"Jennifer, what are you doing here?"

The next morning, Sheree danced into Ravenwood High, a smile across her face, humming a song through the hall. She stopped at her locker and undid the combination to open it. A few lockers down, Jennifer was pulling a large textbook out. So lost in her own happiness, Sheree didn't seem to notice Jennifer's solemn face.

"Hi Jen! You really scared me last night. I'm sure glad that you found your earring. I bet you forgot it when…"

But Jennifer interrupted Sheree, her voice trembling. "You haven't heard, have you?"

Looking at Jennifer now with serious, questioning eyes, Sheree asked, "Heard what?"

Jennifer was about to speak, but instead put her hand over her mouth, trying to stifle back the tears that were trying to escape. *She looks so happy. I can't tell her. I just can't.*

"What is it Jennifer, tell me?" Sheree interrogated, worried about what it was, not having any idea what was going on.

A large lump formed in Jennifer's throat as she dropped her bag and said, "Jeff was in a car accident last night."

"Oh my gawd. Is he all right?" she asked clutching her locket, expecting the answer to be yes, her eyes wide with fear.

A tear that Jennifer had tried so hard to keep in, finally escaped her eye. "No, he's not. I'm sorry, Sheree, I'm so sorry," she said with her arms outstretched, reaching over to give Sheree a hug, loud sobs coming from her. "He's dead."

Chapter 8
It's Back

"He's… dead?"

Her face became pale, the blood rushing out of her head; turning white as a ghost. Anger and sadness intertwined; her stomach twisting and turning; unanswerable questions crossing her mind.

Blank.

Nothing.

Shock.

Slamming her locker door, she went straight down the hall and into her first period Biology class in room 306. It took her longer than usual to sit down at her desk, seemingly unable to walk without bumping into her surroundings. Her expression remained unchanged. The bell rang, making Sheree's head throb with pain. It seemed like it would never end, a continuous obnoxious noise.

Mr. O' Neill turned his attention to the class. "Please open your books to page…"

But Sheree couldn't take it any more. She ran out of the classroom crying and screaming, leaving her books and bag behind her as the teacher and students stopped what they were doing to watch Sheree run frantically through the hall. Suddenly she stopped, dropping to her knees. Without warning, she vomited on the mismatched vinyl tiles, a few more students from other classrooms looking out to see what the commotion was.

A teacher was about to approach Sheree when Jennifer ran up to her. "Come on," she said, bending down and putting Sheree's arm around her neck before standing up, hoping that she had enough strength to lift her. They walked to the main office, where Jennifer explained everything to the principal. Sheree looked numb, staring blankly at the air.

"Do you want to talk to a counselor?" Mr. Blaire, a descendant of the town's founder and principal of Ravenwood High School, asked Sheree.

There was no answer.

"She looks like she's gone into shock," the principal deducted. "Let me call her parents so they can take her home."

Nodding her head with approval, Jennifer suddenly realized something. "Wait, they're probably at the hospital."

"The hospital? What for?" he asked, putting his phone down.

"Her brother Brendon had an accident, fell out of a tree. Sheree told me he'll be there at least until tomorrow because they're worried about a concussion or something," Jennifer informed the principal.

Rubbing his chin with his forefinger and thumb, Mr. Blaire appeared to be trying to come up with a solution when Jennifer offered one.

"I could call my mom and see if she could take her home."

Nodding, he said back, "You should go with her. She shouldn't be alone if she's taking Mr. Mains's death this hard. Such a shame, he was one of my favorite students. Tragedies like this just shouldn't happen."

Agreeing to the principal's suggestion, Jennifer called her mother to pick them up. It seemed to take an eternity for her mom to arrive, and even longer for her to make sure it was okay for her daughter to miss a day of school. After Mr. Blaire assured her that he was the one who okayed the absence, Mrs. Hoang finally agreed to take them to Sheree's house.

The car ride was silent, the radio was off, and there was a hint of what smelled like old urine emanating from the upholstery. When they had pulled onto Song's End, Jennifer took notice of the few stately mansions on the street, especially the first one on the corner where it connected to Main Street. It was Blaire House, and she wondered if the principal lived there. It was something she had never really concerned herself with before, but was suddenly curious about. There was a high flagpole with a large American flag waving in the air on the corner of the lot, and on the side of the yellow and white mansion was a smaller American flag attached to one side of the wrap around porch where the front entrance was, a Washington State flag on the other side of it.

They passed many other houses, since Sheree lived toward the end of the street by the cemetery, and Jennifer noticed that, with the exception of the few mansions, the rest of the houses looked cookie-cutter, like they were all from the same blueprint. There were some minor differences. Some had different entrances or a covered wrap around porch like the larger manors on the street, and some had even added garages or converted some of the interior space into one. For some reason or another, she was suddenly aware that Sheree's house was identical in almost every way as her boyfriend Chad's house, the only difference being a heavy presence of orange in his rather than avocado. Perhaps it was the fact that they had just passed his house that brought this realization to her. Or perhaps it was just a way to try and get her mind off of the fact that one of her friends had just died the night before.

After they pulled into the Hollins's driveway, Jennifer got out of the car and opened the back door, offering her hand to help Sheree out. Waving her mom goodbye, Jennifer turned around and reached for the doorknob, not even thinking to unlock the door first. Surprised, she found that it was already unlocked, and figured that Sheree's parents must have been too preoccupied to remember to lock it before leaving the house, much like the night before when she was able to get in to look for her earring she'd forgotten when she spent the night last.

It was like Sheree was a zombie as Jennifer led her up the stairs toward her bedroom. Trying to steady both herself and her friend, she was scared they'd fall. Then, as if waking from a trance, Sheree started crying again as she saw Jeff's letterman jacket lying on top of her bed, the faint scent of Obsession quietly filling the air.

"The itsy bitsy spider went up the water spout…"

Sheree's eyes fluttered like butterfly wings as she heard the soft sound again for the first time in weeks.

"Down came the rain and washed the spider out…"

Looking outside from the bay window in her room, she saw that it was pouring down rain. Thunder was roaring and rumbling, and lightning flashing, pushing its way through the window like a strobe light and casting eerie shadows.

"Jeff is gone and Brendon's out of the way…
Now it's time for Jen and I to go outside and play!"

"Noooooooo!"

Was that me who just screamed?

Without delay, Sheree quickly picked up her pink princess phone on her bedside table and dialed Jennifer's number. One ring. Two rings. Three rings.

Why isn't she answering?

Four rings. Five rings. Six rings.

A frightening thought went into her mind. What if the thing that has been haunting her was with Jennifer right now? Jennifer could be hurt. She could be… dead.

Nine rings. Ten rings.

"Hello?" Sheree heard faintly on the other line.

"Oh, Jennifer, you're okay," Sheree said with a sigh of relief.

Lifting the phone closer to her ear, Jennifer asked sleepily, "Sheree? What are you talking about?"

"I thought, I thought…" she stopped herself from saying what she wanted to tell her friend. *I thought you were dead.*

"What do you want?" Jennifer insisted.

"Oh, it was nothing," Sheree lied.

A brief pause.

"Sheree, you called me at, are you frickin' kidding me, two-thirty in the morning to see if I was okay? I'm not buying it," Jennifer told her, trying not to sound annoyed but finding it difficult to hide, sitting up in her bed. "Tell me what you really called for. Did you think something happened to me?"

"Well…" Sheree hesitated. "I heard the voice from my vent again."

"Oh." Not sure how to respond, it was the only thing Jennifer could say.

"I think that whoever or whatever is saying those things is also the one who pushed Brendon off the branch and…"

"He fell off the branch, he wasn't pushed," Jennifer said, interrupting her.

Her voice sounded so shrill. So… evil.

"What did you mean by that?"

"He fell off that branch. Nobody pushed him."

"But Brendon told me…"

"I don't care what Brendon said. He wasn't pushed."

Why was she being so defensive? Why wouldn't she listen to what Sheree was trying to tell her? Why, after being so nice and caring earlier that day, was she now being so mean?

"I'm sorry, it's late and I'm still a bit groggy and cranky. It's just… it was an accident. You know that. It's easy for the mind to imagine things to make sense of a terrible situation."

"You're right. Why would someone want to kill Brendon?"

After waking from another mostly sleepless night, Sheree walked out of her bedroom and downstairs to eat breakfast. It was unusually quiet, but that was because Brendon wasn't there, she knew. The last couple days had been calm since he was in the hospital, with the exception of Sheree dealing with the death of her boyfriend, Jeff.

I wonder why they have to keep him there for so long if he only has a few bruises, a broken nose and a fractured arm.

After much mental debate, she decided that it was for the money. As she descended from the stairs, she overheard her parents talking. They seemed to be in a very serious conversation. Standing a few steps from the bottom of the staircase, she tried to listen to what they were saying.

"This is getting ridiculous. Why do they have to continue to keep Brendon in the hospital?" Mr. Hollins wondered.

"I'm not sure why," Mrs. Hollins said, shaking her head, "I'm not sure."

"I already see him every day, I mean, hell, I work in the morgue down in the basement of the hospital, but come on. You're a nurse, and although you haven't practiced since… well, it's not like he wouldn't be in capable hands," her father said, shaking his head before it got even redder with anger. "Do they think that we are made of money? We can't afford to keep him in there if he's only got a fractured arm and a broken nose, especially not on the shitty insurance us in the healthcare profession get! Why won't they let us take him home?"

Not sure why her father was asking all these questions to the one person he knew couldn't answer them was somewhat unnerving. It was like asking a cat to clean out its own litter box, which, now that Sheree thought about it, her father had done years ago when they owned a cat. It had the same fate as her sister.

The telephone rang, startling Sheree. Her father answered the phone before it had even finished with its initial ringtone, and she assured herself that now would be a good time to go into the kitchen and eat. "Morning Mom, morning Dad," she said as she entered the kitchen and took out a box of Cheerios from the cupboard, inspecting its contents and making sure this box didn't have any spiders in it before pouring herself a bowl, regretting not grabbing the box of Lucky Charms instead after covering the cereal with milk.

Walking over toward her daughter, Mrs. Hollins gave Sheree a hug from behind, reassuring her that everything will be all right. Smiling back, Sheree wanted very much to say 'thank you' but knew that words would only screw up the sentimental gesture.

"Thank you very much," her dad said into the receiver before hanging up the telephone.

"Who was that?" Sheree asked, spooning a bite of cereal.

"It was the hospital," he informed his daughter and wife. "They said that Brendon is ready to come home now."

Well it's about time!

"That's great!" she said enthusiastically.

Wait. Do I really want him to come home? What if the evil still wants Brendon out of its way? It might try to kill him. Again!

"Jennifer! Wait up!" Sheree called, running toward her friend.

Turning around to see who yelled for her, Jennifer smiled and waved when she saw Sheree. *Oh Sweet Buddha, she looks like a penguin when she runs.* She couldn't help but laugh at the sight.

"What are you laughing at?" Sheree demanded, having caught up to Jennifer.

"You!"

"Me?"

"Yes you," Jennifer said. "You waddle when you run, and that outfit really makes you look like a penguin!"

Suddenly self-conscious, Sheree inspected her wardrobe; a white shirt, black cardigan sweater, black pants and happy-ass yellow flats. "Holy crap, I do look like a penguin!"

"What the hell were you thinking when you put on those shoes?" Jennifer asked, her face all scrunched up in a not-so-attractive way. "I mean, if you would've worn black shoes, the whole outfit wouldn't stand out so much, but yellow?"

"What am I going to do?" Sheree wondered, frightened beyond all belief. "I'm the head of the Fashion Committee and I'm committing one of the most heinous crimes imaginable! Courtney will so call dibs on my seat if she sees me like this!"

"Courtney does have it out for you. I mean, isn't she the reason you aren't a cheerleader?" Jennifer asked, but knowing the answer was a resounding YES!

"Shit."

Thinking quickly, Jennifer came up with an excuse. "I've got it! You're dressing like a penguin to raise money for the zoo!"

"That's brilliant!" Sheree exclaimed.

"Oh!" Jennifer added, rummaging through her purse. "I'm wearing my leopard print blouse, here," she said, handing Sheree her eyeliner pen, "paint some whiskers on my cheeks and blacken a small spot on my nose!"

They walked into Ravenwood High, dressed and looking like a couple of freaks, laughing through the halls as people stared at them wondering what they were thinking.

"It's for the zoo," they yelled over and over as students and teachers asked.

It feels so good to laugh. I'm so tired of crying. I don't want to cry anymore. I don't even want to think about Jeff. Just have a good day, Sheree.

Chapter 9
The Funeral

Before Sheree realized it, Saturday had arrived. Normally she looked forward to Saturdays, being the only truly free day of the week; no restrictions; no rules; no school or bedtime. However today was one she had dreaded all week because it was the day the Mains family was going to bury their only child, Jeff.

As if in a trance, she proceeded to get ready for the funeral, thankful that she chose her outfit the night before so she'd avoid another penguin incident. After getting dressed and made up, she walked down the stairs and into the kitchen where her mother and father were already dressed as well, both staring at the espresso machine, waiting silently for the coffee to enter the carafe. Being that her stomach was somewhat in knots, she decided not to eat, but when her mom offered one of her famous hazelnut cold coffees, she couldn't refuse. It was a drink that could be consumed rapidly since the hot coffee was only cooled by hazelnut flavored half-and-half and milk, and one that gave an instant boost in energy. When she lowered the empty glass from her mouth, she saw her plump brother, having unsuccessfully dressed himself with his new sling holding his arm toward his midsection, staring back at her. Their mother quickly made her way over to him to help.

"Oh, what am I going to do with you!" she proclaimed, adjusting and readjusting his dress shirt and jacket.

"OW! Stop Mom, you're hurting me!" Brendon screamed, his eyes wider than Sheree had ever seen them. "I'm all broken, remember?!"

Apologizing and kissing, their mother continued to correct the wardrobe malfunction until it was decently remedied to reveal a fairly handsome outfit. *Too bad Brendon's wearing it, or it might look better,* Sheree thought to herself, smirking.

As if Brendon had heard her thoughts, he gave her a dirty look that said 'punk.'

What the hell? Are my thoughts so transparent anyone can see them? Or am I actually saying them aloud and don't realize it? I mean, everyone already thinks I'm crazy for hearing voices and seeing imaginary spiders, so maybe this isn't such a far-fetched conclusion to make, right?

Noticing that the other three members of her family were busy ignoring her, she decided that she wasn't really talking out her thoughts, but maybe her facial expressions were speaking for themselves, which very well could be the case since she could create the most comprehensive expressions imaginable that anyone could figure out what she was thinking at a given moment if they knew her well enough. That or she truly was a telepath and was inadvertently sending her thoughts to her recipients.

After rinsing out her glass, smiling at the happy cow on the front of it and placing it next to the sink, she rushed upstairs to brush her teeth before they had to leave. Turning on the faucet suddenly struck a cord with her, and her body seemed to awaken as her bladder informed her it had to be emptied. Now. Anxiety pee, she called it; the kind that never seemed to relinquish its urgency, no matter how many times she went. When she had finished brushing her teeth, she went again, and could swear that she still had to go another time, but told herself that the mind is more powerful than the urethra. Remembering to grab a few things out of her room, she quickly picked them up and rushed back down the stairs yelling, "Hurry up guys or we're going to be late!"

"Usually an only child would end up spoiled and without manners and politeness… but not Jeff," the pastor said, beginning the service at the Ravenwood First Congregational Church. "His parents are upstanding members of the Ravenwood community, and as such, had raised their son to be one as well, taking him to all of the same charity functions and town meetings and the annual Mayor's Ball they attended, all of which required proper etiquette and respect for people in all positions and status. They not only taught him social skills, but community responsibility and the importance of keeping one's mind and body fit by introducing books and reading and art and exercise at a very early age. By the time he entered kindergarten, he had already been exposed to more culture than most people experience in a lifetime. He was also allowed to explore his interests without censor, something most parents would feel quite uncomfortable about with all of the colorful information available, which in turn brought him a truer sense of self and spirituality that many people twice his age have yet to comprehend.

"Jeff was also a very active individual, having played every position in baseball and mastering each, however his love of soccer overshadowed even that. His talent on the field was only matched by his intellect. Football, he liked to call it, and as every other country except America does, was his passion, and he played with his heart and soul.

"And recently, as his parents discovered after Jeff had fallen in love with a young schoolmate, was his ability to write poetry. Apparently he had never taken an interest in writing until he met this young girl, and his parents have requested her to read one of the poems he had given her. Sheree, if you'll please…"

Almost shocked at the calling of her name, Sheree quickly remembered why she had been holding onto the piece of paper in her hand. As she made her way up to the podium, she wiped away her tears with a tissue. The pastor took a seat on a bench just a few feet away, but not with the rest of the gathering. Placing the folded stationary onto the podium, she looked at the crowd of people there to honor her dead boyfriend. It seemed like there were hundreds of people from family, to friends and acquaintances, and even the mayor and his family. Everyone who knew and loved him was there, which for Jeff was probably everyone he had ever met. Giving his parents a quaint smile, she prayed she would be able to read and finish the beautiful poem without breaking into a cry. Unfolding the paper, she looked at the audience once more before reading:

My eyes have never seen radiant beauty
nor my heart or my soul
with you I am complete
with you I am unbroken

Thinking of a day without you makes me crumble
the thought unbearable
I cannot ponder
a more terrible thing

But I am awakened by your sunlight
a smile inspirational
laughter so free
and wild and insatiable

Through your eyes come visions of our lives together
and know you feel the same
maybe more so
since you saw it in mine first.

The rows of people were silent and she realized that tears were streaking down her face as she folded the poem back in half and again. Walking toward her seat next to her parents and brother, Jeff's mother stood, her arms outstretched and waiting for Sheree, who went in for the comforting hug she was offering.

"Thank you, Sheree," she whispered into her ear in a broken speech. When the two finished their embrace and seated themselves, the pastor resumed his position at the podium.

"As anyone can tell you, Jeffrey Mains touched everyone he met with his willingness to listen, learn, live and lend a helping hand when needed. His charm and spirit was undeniable, and you couldn't help but feel a breath of fresh air when he entered a room. Scripture tells us in 1st Timothy 6:17 that God gives us richly all things to enjoy and Jeff took this to heart. He lived his life to its fullest, having experienced so much in a short span of time, and taking in all God has to offer in this world, taking advice from such gurus as Eeyore in the classic children's book, Winnie-the-Pooh, when he said, "We can't all, and some of us don't. That's all there is to it." and Dr. Seuss in The Lorax, "UNLESS someone like you cares a whole awful lot, nothing is going to get better. It's not." These simple stories tell us of some of life's most important lessons; cherishing diversity; respecting everybody's right to live their own life; friends can get you through anything.

"Let us pray. Dear Heavenly Creator, though we do not understand why you have taken Jeffrey away at such a young age, we know that he is in your house with you, probably looking down at all of us gathered to honor his life and telling us not to be sad or hurt or angry. And while it is okay to feel such emotions during this process of grief, let us instead focus our energy on all the joy he has brought into each of our lives, and live our own lives as fully as he did. Jesus, I pray that Your love will comfort us during this time of sorrow, which for some of us has already passed, and others has yet to come. In Your name we pray. Amen.

"We all grieve differently, and because of this, we may have days when we feel good, and others where we don't. Jeff treated everyone as if they were family, and I hope that you can all take comfort in each other in your times of need, whether it be a much needed hug or a listening ear or even just the company of a friend."

Placing his hands on either side of the podium, he paused for a few moments, ineffectively stifling what were clearly tears. He pulled from his pocket a simple red handkerchief and dried his eyes before continuing the service. "In a few moments, we will allow those of you who wish to say their final goodbyes to Jeff a chance to do so. Please wait for the usher to reach your row to excuse you, at which time you can come up to the casket for viewing, or make your way to the reception room for refreshments and all of Jeff's favorite cookies. And if you haven't done so already, please remember to sign the guest book before you leave today. May God's peace be with all of you."

And with that, the service was over. From the front row, Sheree peered around and watched as people split off in two directions, noticing who was walking up to the casket for a final viewing, and those heading straight to the lobby and reception area. There didn't appear to be a rhyme or reason as to who was going in either direction, and as Sheree pondered the thought, she suddenly realized that it didn't matter. After what seemed an eternity of waiting for the usher to reach the first row, being that the church's seats were full, and some people had been standing in the back because of that, he finally approached them, gesturing with his hand for them to stand up and leave their seats. For as long as she could remember, she couldn't handle being near a dead body even though it was her father's profession, and even as she stood up and started walking toward the casket, following Jeff's parents with a bit of distance between them, the thought that Jeff was indeed dead had somehow escaped her in the last few seconds.

Then she stopped. Halfway up to the casket, she stood still, staring at the people in front of her, people she didn't even know looking at him in the beautiful monochromatically painted mural of a soaring hawk above a forested mountain scenery surrounding the casket, then watching as his mother and father looked over their son, her cries unintentionally loud and his arm around her trying to be strong for her sake. As Mr. Mains led his wife away, she somehow found the courage to continue walking toward Jeff, and when she saw his face, she couldn't help but cry too. Through her tears she could see faint imperfections on his face, his skin covered in makeup to hide where the glass from the driver's side window of his car struck him, and the thought of wanting to find out who did the work so she could thank them wandered into her mind. Then she did something completely unexpected, nearly expelling all her fears of being around death she previously had. Leaning toward the body, she closed her eyes and kissed his lips, no longer warm and moist, but cold and dry. As she lifted herself from him, she said, "I will always love you," in an almost inaudible voice, reopening her eyes to find a few astonished people behind her as they waited their turn for viewing.

Carefully avoiding any judgmental stares, she made her way to the lobby and toward her family, but was stopped by a hand grasping her shoulder, causing her to turn around to find Mrs. Mains, her expression unreadable. *Oh gawd, she saw what I did and now she's furious!* Sheree thought as fear ran through her body. But then her bloodshot eyes lit up, along with her tear stained face to reveal a smile, and with her hand still on Sheree's shoulder, she pulled her in closer for another hug, which a much relieved Sheree reciprocated, so glad that she hadn't offended her.

"I'm so glad Jeff got to know you," Mrs. Mains told her as she backed away, letting her arms drop to her side. "I know we've only met a couple times, but I also know that you made Jeff happy, very happy actually. And I also believe that, and I don't know if he ever told you this, he was in love with you."

Wiping the tears that didn't seem to want to dissipate from her eyes, she said, "He did tell me, and show me, and I am so in love with him still!"

She smiled again. "I know this must be hard for you, but I am thankful that he was able to experience love, true love, with you, and my husband and I were wondering if you could attend the graveside service with us. We are keeping it small, very private, just our parents and ourselves, but we would like you to be there too."

Unable to speak, Sheree nodded her acceptance to the offer.

"Good. Now go get yourself some cookies and something to drink. My mother and I were up all last night baking them because Jeff had always said that when he died..." she paused briefly. "That when he died, he wanted people to not grieve over his death, but just enjoy his favorite cookies!"

Without control, Sheree burst into laughter because that sounded exactly like something Jeff would say, joined by Mrs. Mains, both of whom were being stared at with confusion by the large crowd of people, most holding a Styrofoam cup filled with juice or milk or coffee in one hand and a half eaten cookie in the other.

Chapter 10
A Gift from the Grave

"I told you to stop asking me stupid questions, Brendon!" Sheree shouted to her brother, turning around to face him with ferocious eyes, her face burning with anger.

His deep brown eyes looked at her, like a sad little puppy. "I'm sorry, Sheree. I guess that I'm just… curious."

Nine.

What a year. He's always got to know what's happening. What this is and that and how, why, when, where, who?! Sheree thought as she walked through the dark unwelcoming entrance of the forest. Brendon followed closely.

Sheree hadn't ever wandered into the forest that essentially was her backyard, and decided that since it was a fairly warm late autumn afternoon, she'd try to get over her recent fear and enjoy the venture. On the other hand, Brendon was always in the forest after school when it wasn't raining, and most of the time on the weekends too, playing with friends, building forts, and pretending to be Super Samurai Slugs or whatever the latest kid's television slash comic book slash toy slash video game combo was cool at the moment.

While carefully treading through the vast amount of cluttered trees, Sheree noticed that this part of the forest was much more open than the one in Ravenwood Park, giving her a sigh of relief. Casually following what looked like a well-worn trail, she remembered her brother's "what if…" stage. What if this, what if that, what if what if what if! It seemed the questions became more and more absurd each time. Noticing a fallen tree, she lifted her legs to get over it, not knowing if she'd be able to reach the other side. It probably would have been more intelligent to step onto the log then jump down to the other side, but that would have been too easy and it always seemed like Sheree enjoyed making things harder for herself. As she looked down to see if her other foot was going to make it, she saw that her shoe was loosely tied. Straddling the tree like a pony, she looked over to her other shoe and it wasn't tied at all, the white laces caked with mud. *Not the smartest thing to do when walking in the woods,* Sheree realized, lifting her other leg over. After tying both shoelaces tightly, she wiped the excess dirt onto her blue jeans, figuring that nobody from the fashion committee would catch her out here in the secluded forest.

"What if…"

Oh no. Here we go again. It's your fault, you know. Dammit. If you hadn't suddenly thought about it, this wouldn't have happened.

Her eyes rolled in disbelief.

"What if…" Brendon continued, "…a tree fell over and landed on me?"

"Then you'll die," Sheree told him, giving him a cold stare. "Unless, of course, you fall out of the tree first, then you might die before it hit you."

"That's not funny, jerk," he said, scowling at her, rubbing his arm that he'd fractured almost two months ago.

Laughing, Sheree said, "On the contrary, it's damn right hilarious!"

When she turned around, she had the feeling that something was missing, but what? Her mind was in a deep thought when she suddenly fell to the ground and landed on a large, scattered pile of dead, brittle, brown maple leaves. The decaying leaves rubbing against her face irritated her sensitive skin. After sitting up, she brushed a few leaves out of her soft strawberry-blond hair with soiled hands, streaking the strands with brown lowlights unintentionally.

"My necklace!" Sheree screamed, feeling the spot on her neck that the locket she normally wore was supposed to be. "Brendon, you have to help me look for my necklace. You have to!"

Looking around, she noticed that Brendon was nowhere in sight. A cold shock of fear tremulously ran through her body like a bolt of electricity. The air began to get heavy. Heavier and heavier with every breath her lungs took in; the air felt as though it was thick molasses instead of precious nitrogen and oxygen.

Heavier.

Heavier until she could barely breathe, unable to take in the breath she needed so desperately to live.

A cold hand grasped her shoulder.

It felt like death.

She quickly turned around.

"Oh!" she sighed in relief. "There you are. I thought that you ran off and got yourself lost."

Brendon flashed an evil grin.

Why does he keep looking at me like that? Sheree wondered, breathing deeply now that the air had thinned out enough so she could.

His smile faded and he looked serious. "I was unconscious and bleeding."

"And I almost kicked you for scaring me like that!"

"You were going to kick me?"

"I thought you were playing again, like that time in the bathroom when you pretended to be dead and fell out of the cabinet under the sink."

"Fine, I'll give you that. I really thought you were going to kill me after I did what I did while you and Jeff were…"

The mentioning of his name struck a chord in Sheree's body, but didn't really sink in completely… yet.

Realizing his mistake, Brendon quickly apologized. "I'm sorry, so sorry Sheree. I didn't mean to… I…"

"It's okay, really. C'mon, Brendon, will you help me look for my necklace?" It was more of a plea of mercy than a question.

He thought about it for a second. "Hmmm… okay. But only if you'll pay me."

A frown filled Sheree's face. *Should I pay him to look for it? Well, of course. It was the only thing that Jeff gave me before he died…* Sheree's thoughts trailed off.

Jeff.

It had been at least a couple weeks since Sheree had wept over the loss of him. How long was it now, seven, maybe eight weeks since his accident? She couldn't quite remember.

The day it was on the news and in the local paper, Sheree was too busy crying and trying to understand why God would have taken him away from her. Unable to explain why she felt so close and connected to this person whom she had only known for less than a month, yet felt she'd known a lifetime or two or three. Maybe he was her soul mate, her destiny to be with him and when he was killed, it took a part of her with him. Perhaps it was for the best she didn't know or even want to know all of the details, not once asking her father if he had been the one who received his body. Or perhaps it wasn't. If she knew that it was just a senseless accident that not only killed her boyfriend, but also took the life of another driver, paralyzing the passenger in that car too, and not supernatural, as the twisted lullaby that she had heard later that night suggested, it may have helped her be more at peace with the situation.

It's amazing just how blind to the truth we can make ourselves be.

His face flashed into her mind. His perfect face. His gorgeous, short brown hair. His unbelievably clear blue eyes, so caring and forgiving. The image was enough to bring back all the joy she had felt when he was with her. But it didn't last. Brendon's voice broke into her daydream, causing the vision to fade. "What was that?"

He rolled his puppy dog eyes. "I said, is it a deal or not?" his teeth clenched together as he repeated the question.

"How much do you want?" Sheree asked, hoping that it would be reasonable, but knowing her brother it would be probably be some outrageous amount.

"A buck."

"Deal," Sheree said quickly. Almost too quickly, she thought, as she reached into her jean pocket and pulled out a crumpled one-dollar bill.

Greedily, Brendon snatched it from her hand, stuffed it in his jean pocket, and started looking for the necklace. "It's that locket you always wear, right?" he asked, making sure he knew exactly what it was she was looking for.

"That's the one," she told him, her hands beginning to search through the moist dirt, the tiny clumps of brown soil clinging to the inside of her fingernails. Fifty dollars, that's how much the Regal Nail Salon charged for the fake nails she had gotten just last weekend with Jen, and now, as she felt around the damp filth for her lost locket, particles finding their way into the tiniest of crevices, it was fifty dollars well spent. Those claws were like five tiny shovels a hand, managing to dig up more dirt than she really needed to, and not one of them breaking off. Oh, if all those little Vietnamese women who worked on them could see what she was doing with them now, they'd probably faint. After rummaging through the dirt for ten minutes and neither of them finding anything, Sheree was about to lose all hope of locating the chain when a golden strand caught her eyes. Without more ado, she rushed over to the strand and dug her hand into the soft dirt to retrieve it.

She gripped the object.

It felt slimy.

Cold and slimy.

Quickly, Sheree threw it down when she realized it was a worm, long, slim and golden in color like the locket's chain. After wiping her dirty hands off on her faded blue denim jeans, she told Brendon she was giving up the search and heading home.

"Are you sure?" he asked, lifting his hands out of a pile of leaves he had been thoroughly looking through. "That locket means a lot to you, I'll keep looking. It's gotta be around here somewhere. Don't worry, I'll find it."

Somewhat taken aback by her brother's sincerity, she smiled. "Thank you, but don't worry about it."

"But…"

"Its okay, Bren. I'll be fine."

Reaching into his pocket with his mud-coated hands, he pulled out the crumpled one-dollar bill. "We didn't find it, so here's your money back."

"Keep it. The deal was that you would help me, and you did," she told him, bending down to give him a hug.

"Sheree, I…" Brendon started to say, but broke off.

"What is it?" Sheree asked, wondering what was on his mind.

Shaking his head and giggling, he told her, "Never mind, it's nothing."

They were both covered in mud and knew their mother was going to have a conniption when she saw the two of them walk into the house, reddish-brown sludge enveloping every square inch of their bodies. Knowing their mom, Sheree thought that she'd probably make them go hose off in the backyard before letting them in to change into some dry, clean clothes. Sure enough, she was right.

※ ※ ※

"Mom, I'm going to the cemetery," Sheree called from the entryway of the old creepy house on Song's End that she called home, her long winter coat already on.

After her mom nodded her acknowledgement, Sheree opened the ancient door and went out into the frigid late fall night, such a contrast from the warm day just a few hours prior. The old cemetery where Jeff was buried was only a few houses down from her home, and she didn't have to walk to see it. The view from her bedroom's bay window framed it on one side, giving her a full outlook of the cemetery; the large wrought iron fence encasing it; the unused caretaker's shack; the hundreds, maybe thousands of stone and concrete markers, some of which were elaborate statues that, in another setting, would be considered works of art.

The funeral was the same night as Ravenwood's Homecoming game and dance. It was to be their next date, and ironically it would be their last, when Sheree reluctantly said goodbye to Jeff as he lay cold and frozen in a casket. Right after the funeral, Sheree went there every night after dinner. And during that time she would spend hours just crying and talking to him, hoping that he could hear her from beyond the grave. That's how it was… for the first week. Then she started getting on with her life, spending more time with Jennifer and her family, and the visits became shorter and less frequent until one day they altogether stopped.

She walked right up to the tombstone.

JEFFREY WILLIAM MAINS

It had been nearly a month since she last went to the gravesite, she realized. Hot tears ran down her cool cheeks causing her vision to blur, everything losing focus. Hadn't she cried enough? Hadn't she gotten over the fact that he was never going to be with her, or hold her, or kiss her ever again? She cried for an entire week after the funeral, crying and crying until all of her tears were dried up. With the sleeve of her wool jacket, she wiped away the teardrops from her face, immediately regretting it as her cheek began to itch from the reaction with the wool.

Reaching into the pocket of her coat, she pulled out a purple wild flower that she had picked earlier that day in the woods on her way home, and carefully placed it down in front of the protruding granite stone. Decayed flowers lined the grave, indicating that she wasn't alone in the decreased visitation department. Cursing herself for living and forgetting about the person she thought she was going to marry and spend the rest of her life with, she let out a loud howl that seemed to echo through the graveyard, startling a few crows from their perch in the tree beside her. The sight of the dead flowers over the grave was unbearable, so she picked them up in bundles and threw them away from her sight, not noticing that they were piling in front of other burial markers.

Startled, she stopped what she was doing. Her eyes fixed on something that was lying over the ground on the gravesite just underneath all of the rotting vegetation. A confused expression formed on her face as she lifted the gold chain. It was her necklace, the locket that she had lost in the forest earlier that day. Upon opening it she saw, there tucked away in the small compartment, the picture of her and Jeff on their first date. It was unbelievable, and the only explanation she could come up with was impossible. With her eyes closed, she stood up, holding onto the locket with both hands as she did so, her head bowing toward the stone.

"Thank you, Jeff."

Chapter 11
Revelations

It was two weeks until Christmas, three weeks until the end of the world according to some Y2K apocalypse theorists's prophecies that were all the rage and taking up more news coverage than, say, actual news, and Sheree was more stressed out than ever. All of her teachers seemed to be giving out homework like it was candy (the kind that sticks together when you try to pull out just one from the jar at grandma's house because she left it in an open bowl on the coffee table for moisture to creep over and create a new lifeform), her parents decided that she needed to do more chores around the house, and her favorite new sitcom was suddenly canceled without any explanation. On top of all that, the weather changed drastically overnight. The week before was beautiful and warm, the whole reason she decided to take a walk into the forest with her brother, but now it was cold and snowing as she looked out her bay window, sitting on the bench in the nook, her arms wrapped around her knees as she stared at the cemetery where her boyfriend was laid to rest.

"Northwest weather is so unpredictable!" she said to herself. After pondering all the bad stuff going on in her life and wondering if this really was the end times, she was thankful for one thing… she hadn't heard that awful voice singing to her in the middle of the night for over two months. In fact, now that she had thought about it, the voice and all the crazy incidents that went along with it hadn't manifested themselves since the day after Jeff died. Deciding that it was only a coincidence, she brushed off the thought that Jeff had anything to do with the paranormal disturbance's abrupt disappearance.

Having been so frustrated lately, Sheree decided that a nice, long, hot shower would help her relax. Most people would take a bath to unwind, but since a near drowning experience at the beach when she was six, she hadn't been able to submerge her body in water without trembling to the verge of convulsion. Bath time after that was like Danny Pintauro's seizures in the movie *Cujo*. Contrary to that, all the seawater she had swallowed had somehow altered her taste. She had gone from a sugar-loving water-baby to a salt-craving claustrohydrophobic. Although technically she really didn't have a phobia, but a tangible reason for having a fear of being underwater, she found it easier to say she did rather than explain her ordeal and have to relive that nightmare again.

After locking the bathroom door, she undressed, setting her clothes on the counter next to the sink. A sock fell to the ground but Sheree didn't notice. The water took a while to warm up as she held her hand under the faucet in the bathtub after turning the hot water on. Once it became hotter than she could manage, she turned on the cold water just enough to make it bearable and lifted the nozzle to start the shower, stepping in a few seconds later. Steam rose up and quickly filled the room as Sheree rinsed her hair under the shower, letting the water splash onto her face like sweltering rain. Turning herself around, she wet her entire body, which was getting redder like a boiling lobster. Lathering shampoo through her yellow mane, soap began trickling over her face as she thought, with her eyes closed, about relaxing images of streams and soft winds blowing through a flowering meadow. It was at that moment she began hearing that horrific voice again.

"The itsy bitsy spider went up the water spout…"

Her eyes shot open, stinging almost instantly as the soapy bubbles worked their way into her sockets. Lunging her face into the stream of the showerhead and frantically rinsing away the suds from her face and hair, she thought, *This is not happening, not again!* But it was.

"Down came the rain and washed the spider out…"

Every time she opened her eyes, they closed again with pain. The shampoo not rinsing out of her hair and off her face fast enough, as if it was multiplying. Warm tears began welling up, but did little to help the situation.

"Dead without a body her spirit still remains…
…and the itsy bitsy spider is about to kill again!"

At this, the water went icy cold and Sheree saw what looked like a reflection of herself flash before her, causing her to leap back and almost hurdle out of the shower. The image was hideous and terrifying, almost… subhuman. However dreadful it was, she could definitely tell it was herself. Maybe it was all in her head. Could it be that her unconscious mind was getting the best of her? What else could explain the fact that after two months of nothing, the voice returned just after she realized she hadn't heard it in a while?

"Sorry!" she heard Brendon yell, muffled from both the distance and the closed door. "I didn't know you were in the shower or I would have waited to flush the toilet!"

"Don't worry about it, I was done anyway," Sheree yelled back, quickly toweling off and redressing, terrified that she was losing her mind, but at least thankful that there was an explanation for the rush of cold water, if nothing else. Opening the bathroom door, she nearly toppled back as she saw Brendon standing inches away from it. "Geez Brendon, you scared the shit out of me!" she said to him, gasping with one hand on her chest, her wet hair dripping onto her shirt and down to the floor.

Looking at his sister with a sinister face, he said in his most creepy, monotone voice, "I'm sorry little girl, I didn't mean to frighten you."

"Stop it you freak!" Sheree screamed, closing her ears with her hands. "Make John go away!"

For the past couple years, Brendon had been trying to convince everyone that he had multiple personalities, one-hundred and ninety-two of them to be exact, and he had no control over his actions because he was just a host to all of these characters trapped in his body. One of these personalities, John, was the creepiest one of all. To Sheree, he sounded like a cross between a stalker and a child molester, and it was even more terrifying over the telephone.

"But I like you Sheree, don't you like me?"

"No!"

"C'mon little girl, don't you want some candy? I've got some in my pocket. It's been in there all day so it's nice and warm. If you want it, you just have to reach in and get it."

"STOP!" Sheree shouted, causing their mother to come up stairs to see what all the commotion was about.

"What in the hell is going on here?" Mrs. Hollins inquired, hands on her hips and furious beyond belief.

Still in character, Brendon told her, "I was just offering Sheree some candy."

Cringing, Mrs. Hollins said, "Brendon, knock it off. You know I can't stand it when you use John's voice."

"But this is my voice," the host body of Brendon declared. "If you don't like it, I suggest you stick your head up your ass so you don't have to listen to it."

At this, Mrs. Hollins's face changed immediately to a flaming shade of red, the heat radiating off her and burning into Brendon's flesh. "Go to your room now, Brendon! You're grounded… for a week!"

"What?" Brendon shouted back in his normal voice after what appeared to be a double blink. "Mom, you can't do that, I can't control them! You don't know what it's like having a hundred ninety-two voices in your head all talking at once! You don't know what it feels like to see things so terrible, so twisted that it makes you want to curl up into a fetal position and cry yourself to sleep! To listen to a child sing what sounds like a normal children's lullaby, but morph into a nightmare!"

Unable to comprehend, Sheree was in complete disbelief over what her brother was saying. Maybe she wasn't crazy after all. Maybe all the things she'd been experiencing have been haunting her little brother too.

"Brendon, I'm warning you. If you don't go to your room right now, I'll add another week to that and give all your Christmas presents to charity!" their mother threatened, her face still red and eyes more ferocious than ever.

At this, he closed his open mouth and refrained from saying what he was going to say, instead rushing over to his room, slamming the door behind him. A muffled growl could be heard from his bedroom, which sounded like he was screaming into a pillow.

After her mother's face regained its normal shade, Sheree decided to ask, "Does mental illness run in the family?"

Somewhat shocked by the question, her mother replied, "If you're talking about whether Brendon is crazy or not, trust me, he's just… weird."

Following her mother down the stairs and into the family room, Sheree told her, "Mom, I'm serious. I need to know. It's a school project." It was a lie, but the only one she could come up with on such a short notice.

As if thinking about the question, but obviously looking as though she was trying to stall an answer, her mother declared, "Well, everyone on *my* side of the family has a history of being mentally stable." *Well, most everyone.*

Sheree didn't like the answer she received. "Okay, so what about Dad's?"

"You know, silly thing, that sanity," she said in a sing-song voice. "They sometimes mistake eccentric people for being crazy!"

Sighing and thoroughly annoyed, Sheree folded her arms. "You're dancing around the question, Mother. Can't you just give-it-to-me-straight?" she asked. "Don't you want me to get an A on this project?" she added, hoping that would entice a better response out of her mother.

"Okay, but please don't think too much into this, alright?" Mrs. Hollins requested, sitting herself down onto the frumpy beige family room couch, patting the seat next to her for Sheree to do the same.

Doing as her mother suggested, she sat down and said that she agreed to listen without judgment. Of course, this was just another lie to get her mother to spill everything that she had suspected about her paternal grandmother.

"When you were born, we didn't even know that I was carrying another child, and..."

"I know, I know, because they hadn't even invented X-ray yet, let alone 3D sonograms!" Sheree said laughing, but only for a second that is, until she realized what she'd just done. "Oh, damn it. I just totally dissed myself in the process of trying to dis you. Major suckage."

"Anyway, as I was..."

"No, seriously, how could you not?" Sheree interrupted again, honestly not knowing how something like that was even possible.

Reaching her hand over and touching Sheree's with it, squeezing her fingers, she continued, "I'd only had one ultrasound, and I don't know if the person didn't fully know how to use it, or if Kayla was directly behind you at all times, but we thought we were only having one girl. The image looked a little ghosty to me and your father, like there may have been another child in there with you, but nothing was conclusive. It wasn't until after I had given birth to you that I began to feel labor pains again, and thinking that they were just residual, didn't give it a second thought until a few minutes later, holding you in my arms, the doctor suddenly said, "I see another head coming through!" Everyone in the delivery room was letting out gasps of shock, especially me. I don't even remember pushing with Kayla, and according to the doctor, it was as if she was clawing her own way out of the womb."

"Whoah, I just got a really visual, uh, visual on that. I'm sorry, go on, I won't interrupt again," Sheree assured her mother, shaking her head of the image unsuccessfully, and now trying to build a brick wall in front of it.

Smiling, Mrs. Hollins continued, "Well, to say that it was a complete shock would be an overstatement. According to your grandma Hollins, Frank was destined to have you both. 'Twin girls and a boy, twin girls and a boy. The pin and string technique never lies!' she'd swear. The craziest woman, you're grandmother," her mother concluded before thinking, *Should I tell her about the other boy? No. It's not the right time.*

As if awaiting more, Sheree sat there with an "And?" look on her face. "That's it? That's your story?! That Grandma Hollins swore by her old wives tales, traditions, and superstitions like, oh I don't know, EVERYBODY knows?!" Her arms were wildly flailing around as much as her eyes were.

"Well, yeah," her mother said bluntly.

Rolling her eyes, Sheree shouted, "That's it! I'm going to fail this one for sure! I thought for a moment you were going to tell me that Kayla was possessed by the devil or something. Maybe that's why she ran out into the road in front of that semi and got herself killed!"

There was a pause of silence as her mother stared at her, not believing the words her daughter just spoke. After realizing that her thoughts had transposed into words, Sheree was about to apologize when her mother said quietly, "I thought the same thing."

"WHAT?!" Sheree screamed as she stood up, her thunderous voice reverberating off the walls.

"You would not believe the things that girl would do. She'd sit in her room for hours and talk to some invisible person in a language I've never heard before, and the minute I'd walk in to check up on her, she'd stop talking and slowly turn her head and just look right at me, staring at me with these lifeless eyes and an evil scowl on her face. Sometimes she'd ask to go to the lake, and later on I'd find frog eyes that she would have forgotten to take out of her pocket, along with wild sage and crow's feet. She was a witch by age three, starting to cast spells on your father and I if we didn't give her what she wanted," her mother informed her.

"Holy shit!" Sheree said with complete surprise, somehow forgetting it was her mother she was sitting next to.

"Watch your mouth, young lady!" Mrs. Hollins scolded, sitting back.

Standing back up and pacing back and forth in front of her mother, she chanted over and over, "I can't believe this, I just can't believe this," until she finally said, "She was my sister, my best friend! We did everything together and not once did I see the things you talked about!"

"I'm just kidding!" Mrs. Hollins told her, nervously laughing heartily and actually slapping her knee. "Oh my gawd, you really should have seen the look on your face! I'm telling you, you're too easy to fool."

Still in shock over the whole thing, Sheree queried, "You mean to tell me you were pulling my leg about Kayla?"

"Of course I was. She was the sweetest little girl—besides you—a bit of a tomboy, but there was nothing out-of-the-ordinary with her. Except for her fascination with that doll we got at the Goodwill," her mother said reassuringly though a little apprehensive, standing up and putting her hand on Sheree's shoulder. "Really, you are way too gullible."

"Thanks, Mom." Sheree glared, turning around to head up to her room, letting her mother's hand slip off her shoulder as she walked away. However, an uneasy feeling swept over her and she had to ask one last question. "Why don't we have any pictures of Kayla?"

Her mom's eyes began welling up, just on the verge of tears when she responded, "After she died, a part of me died too. Every time I saw a picture or a toy or anything that reminded me of her, I'd shut down and be unable to function. I got sloppy. I messed up. Ultimately, it's why I am no longer a nurse. After that, your father and I decided it would be best to keep the memories without the constant reminders, so the pictures were all boxed away, her stuff all donated, and all mentioning of her eradicated. It wasn't that we didn't want to know that she once existed, it was just too hard to deal with the realization that she no longer existed. She was gone. When we moved, a part of me wanted to leave that box of pictures with the house she grew up in, but your father convinced me that I would regret it. Don't tell him, but sometimes he is right."

"I didn't know," Sheree said, walking over to hug her mother.

"I just wanted to shelter you from that nightmare, and didn't want you to have to go through the same torment," Mrs. Hollins told her daughter, her words a little broken between sobs. "You saw the whole thing happen and it took years for you to forget."

"I know. I remember it all now like it was yesterday, but it's true, I somehow forgot about her. What kind of monster forgets about her twin sister?" Sheree cried into her mom's shoulder.

Trying her best to comfort Sheree, Mrs. Hollins said back in as calm a voice she could muster, "You are not a monster. You lived. You will go on living. Her death was not your fault. We did everything we could to help you forget, so blame us, not yourself."

For a minute they just held each other. No more words of grief, no more guilt, just a simple act of love: the hug. Sheree started letting her grasp on her mother go and she walked toward the stairs, noticing the three missing posts and wondering when her father would ever fix it. *Maybe I should put some CAUTION tape up or something as a subtle clue. Hmm… where could I get some?*

"Sorry I don't have any mental patients in the family, and don't have any crazy friends either. I hope you find a subject for that project, though," Mrs. Hollins called out.

Turning from the bottom of the staircase, her hand on the rail, she informed her mom, "I lied. There is no project. I just wanted you to tell me if grandma really was insane or not. Really Mom, you are way too gullible."

Smiling, she ran up the stairs to relax to an old book she'd read a dozen times before her father came home and they'd have to go out to dinner and then take all of the Christmas decorations out of storage. However, she first decided to check in on her brother, or John or Allen or Juan Benito or whoever was in charge of Brendon's psyche at the moment, to make sure he was all right.

"Knock, knock," she said as she opened the door, only to find Brendon curled up in a fetal position on his bed, his hands clasping his ears, and the unmistakable voice singing the same twisted song she'd heard so many times before. At first she thought that it was indeed Brendon doing the singing, or one of his many personalities as she had originally suspected over three months ago, but when she walked closer to him, she could clearly hear him crying, "Make it stop, make it stop, make it stop," over and over again.

"Dead without a body her spirit still remains…
…and the itsy bitsy spider is about to kill again!"

It was the same song Sheree had heard only fifteen minutes ago in the shower, and now it was singing to Brendon. How long has this been going on? Has Brendon known about this mysterious presence as long as she has? Was their house really haunted as she had been told by so many people, or was this a particular spirit specifically haunting them?

"Enough with the singing already! When are you going to show yourself?" Sheree threw out, not expecting an answer.

Without warning, the voice shot back, *"Soon!"*

Both Brendon and Sheree jumped back, completely unprepared for the raspy little girl's voice to talk back to them. After the shock wore off, Brendon managed to turn his head towards his sister and say, "You could hear that?"

"I've been hearing twisted lullabies since we moved into this house. It's always "The Itsy Bitsy Spider" and it always ends with something dreadful," Sheree told him, not believing that her brother has probably been going through the same things she had been going through for the past few months.

"Yes!" Brendon said with wild eyes. "I wanted to tell you or Mom or Dad, but I kept getting these random clues to keep quiet."

"Me too!" Sheree cried. "But really, what has it accomplished other than singing scary songs through the air vents? It's probably just a ghost, a spirit that can't rest until something is resolved."

Shaking his head, Brendon seemed to agree. "Hmm, I see your point my dear Watson. So if we figure out what it wants, it'll just go away, right?"

"Possibly, Holmes," Sheree said uncertainly. "I mean, but… how are we going to find out what it wants?"

Getting up off his bed, Brendon said matter-of-factly, "Well that's an easy one, dork. It wants us dead!"

"You're just paranoid, and don't call me a penis," Sheree told him, rolling her eyes and shaking her head. "Name one thing the ghost has done other than sing?"

Clenching his entire body, hands in fists, Brendon shouted, "I'll name three! It knocked you unconscious for a week, pushed me out of a tree, and it killed Jeff!"

"You're crazy," Sheree said to him without giving his opinions much thought. "I was knocked out by a burglar…"

"Who nobody else saw and didn't steal anything," Brendon interrupted, finishing her sentence with his own words. "Penis? Huh?"

Brushing him off again, she continued, "You fell out of the tree, and Jeff died in a car accident. There is nothing supernatural about any of those events, and nothing you say can convince me otherwise."

"Dad's home," Brendon said flatly.

Perplexed, Sheree threw her hands up in the air and yelled, "What?!"

"Dad's home! That means it's pizza time!" Brendon said excitedly doing the Cabbage Patch Dance as pizza was his favorite food. Of course, anything edible was his favorite food, so long as it wasn't pineapple. He quickly ran past his sister and down the stairs to greet their father.

Following her brother, Sheree began chanting, "Daddy's home!" too.

It was a silly tradition, and now that they were in a different house, tradition seemed more important than ever. First they would go out to a pizza dinner and then they'd dig out all of the boxes of Christmas decorations and lights and the already dressed fake tree that they'd had for years and make a night of decorating the inside of the house, listening to the Brenda Lee Christmas album,

The Mormon Tabernacle Choir, and other holiday favorites as they strung lights and hung new ornaments. And then make a day of decorating the outside the next morning, starting with the large multicolored strands of lights around the perimeter of the house, usually having to replace over a third of the bulbs. There was always the chance of the neighbors getting freaked out by their showy display, and possibly their life-sized lighted plastic nativity scene. "It's Christmas! That's Christ! And if you don't like it, I don't give a good goddamn!" their father would shout to anyone who obviously didn't celebrate the season—or at least did so in a more conservative fashion—as he pointed to the blond blue-eyed baby in the manger. This was Sheree's favorite time of the year, and she couldn't wait to make more Christmas memories with her family, even if a horrible evil ghost was haunting her and her brother, and even if they were eating pizza at Ravenwood Bar & Grill where she had her first date with Jeff.

Don't you dare cry, Sheree! Happy memories only!

Sheree faked a smile when the real thing simply could not be conjured.

Why do I always put everything off until the last minute? I've got to stop procrastinating. That'll be my New Year's resolution, Sheree thought to herself, walking down one of the long, wide salt covered sidewalks of the Ravenwood Factory Outlet Shopping Center. Of course, that was her New Year's resolution every year for the last decade, so it was probably going to last as much as most do.

She searched through each store, looking and looking for the perfect gift for everyone on her list, and was able to find stuff for most of them, but she was having trouble with her brother, and with Jennifer. Her dad was easy, especially with a Big Dog store at the outlet center, and her mother's favorite kitchen supply store also had an outlet location there as well. And everyone else was just as easy, but just as she was about to lose all hope of finding a place that could possibly have the perfect gift for Brendon and Jennifer, a big flashy neon sign caught her attention. Everything's A Dollar, the sign read, and while she couldn't quite figure out why that store was in an outlet center, she decided to peruse it anyway. "There's got to be something neat at the dollar store that I can get for Brendon at least," Sheree said quietly as she walked in the direction of Everything's A Dollar, which looked rather crowded from the sidewalk windows.

"Huh, these are cool earrings. I'll get them for Jennifer. Just throw them in a gift bag, she'll never know," she said to herself.

Carefully exploring each aisle of the store inside and out, she finally found a gag gift for Brendon. Before she knew it, her hands were full of useless junk that she planned to get for her family and friends; gizmos and gadgets and tons of plastic odds and ends.

If anyone I know sees me right now, I'm going to die!

Sheree plopped herself down on the floor in a corner of the shop and spread her stuff all over the blue-grey carpet. *What do I not need to buy? Hmm, I'm sure that Mom can live without a decor pickle jar opener. And Dad doesn't really need another coffee mug. And... hell, I don't remember picking any of these out!*

After thoroughly rummaging through the large pile, she left what she didn't want behind a huge cardboard box that had microwavable bowls stacked on top of it, which pretty much consisted of everything that she had found. As she was walking away from her mess, she quickly strode back to the pile, thinking, *Those earrings are just too cute!*

Just as she was about to checkout, Sheree decided to get her wrapping paper and a few gift bags since they were cheap enough at the bargain price of two for a dollar as they were bundled in pairs. *I must go spend crazy when everything in my sight is only a buck,* Sheree thought as she waited for the person in front of her to purchase her stuff. She looked around the store to see if there was anything that she might've missed. The oldies style music made her become sleepy and a loud, surprising yawn escaped her mouth.

"Is that all for you today?"

Blinking and shaking her head a few times for a reality check, Sheree didn't even notice that all of her stuff was already rung up and bagged. "Uh, yeah I am."

"Okay, that'll be eighteen sixty three."

Her eyes opened wide. "Are you sure, that seems like an awful lot?" she asked the clerk who just stared back at her with that I-hate-Christmas-shoppers look on her face. "I'm just kidding!" Sheree said with a smile, pulling out a twenty-dollar bill from her purse. As she waited for her change, she saw a child screaming for a bag of candy his mother was refusing to buy for him.

When she received her change from the clerk, she grabbed her bags and walked outside into the frigid night air, the cold stinging her face from the sudden change. After all the shopping she had done, she was tired and ready to go home.

I'll pick up Brendon's gift tomorrow, she told herself.

As Sheree passed the Pizza Schmizza restaurant located in the same parking lot as the outlet stores, she saw a bunch of kids from Ravenwood High eating and laughing and being plain silly. Recognizing almost all of them, she was about to wave and smile at the people she knew, but she remembered that she was carrying three dollar store bags, a Big Dog bag, a Kitchen Collection bag, and an L.L. Bean bag.

Oh my gawd! Chad Walker is waving me down. Pretend like you don't see him, Sheree. Deciding to avoid any embarrassment from her friends (or that bitch, Courtney) for actually shopping at a store called Everything's A Dollar, she focused on finding her car.

CRUNCH! CRUNCH! CRUNCH!

The snow sounded like cornflakes being crushed as she walked through the well-lit parking lot. Searching the large and very full lot, Sheree couldn't remember where she parked. As she looked in every direction, a relieved appearance formed on her face when she spotted her little blue sedan, now covered with layers of gleaming white snow. "Have I really been here that long?" she asked herself, dropping all of her bags as she fumbled for her keys to open the trunk of the car. She picked them up and carelessly tossed them into the trunk and slammed it down, causing some of the snow to slide off the top of the vehicle and onto the cold ground.

It was only a short drive from the Ravenwood Factory Outlet Shopping Center to her house, as with any distance in the small town, and before she knew it, she was home. The only light coming from the house was the recently decorated Christmas tree in the living room's bay window, strewn with hundreds of lights in every color of the rainbow, and filled with decorations spanning many generations and many childhood projects. Popping the trunk before exiting the car, she strode over to it and began unloading bags, deciding it would be better to make two trips so she could unlock the door without having to drop everything again. Approaching the door, she was expecting the security light to come on, but it never did. *I guess Mom and Dad forgot to flip the switch,* Sheree thought as she pushed the key into the doorknob. After setting the bags down next to the doorway, Sheree flipped the light switch up and walked back out to her car to get the rest of them when she saw someone walk up behind her sedan in the driveway.

"Jennifer!" Sheree screamed as she ran over to her friend, giving her a big bear hug. "Merry Christmas!"

Jennifer looked at her like she was crazy. "What is wrong with you? Are you like some kind of merry ol' Christmas freak or something?"

Almost offended by the comment, Sheree gave Jennifer a light push. She meant for it to be hard, at least hard enough to knock her down onto the snow-covered lawn, but she wasn't strong enough.

"So, what if I am? It is Christmas, and I happen to think that it is a time to be happy."

"Well, I hate Christmas," Jennifer informed her friend. "It's just another day to me. I can't stand it! Everybody all yippee-ay-yay. It makes me sick. We should celebrate Buddhamas instead!"

This is scaring me. She doesn't like Christmas? Who could hate Christmas? And what the hell is Buddhamas?!?

"Okay, so what'd you get me?" Jennifer asked anxiously, eyes wild and excited.

"Whew! For a second there I thought that you were being serious," Sheree said with a sigh of relief.

"I'm only partially serious. My whole family is Buddhist, as most of my people, the Vietnamese people, are," Jennifer told her in a spokesperson-like voice. "But don't tell my mom, I don't believe much of it!" she said quietly with her hand on one side of her mouth as if shielding it from her watchful mother.

"Gotcha," Sheree responded, shaking her head. "Buddhists."

Scrunching her face in that not-so-attractive way, Jennifer asked accusingly, "What about Buddhists?"

Laughing, Sheree responded sarcastically with, "The guy went from one extreme to the next on his quest for enlightenment. How can you not want to emulate him?"

"He was like a nut-a-day eating anorexic model before coming to the conclusion that starving yourself to death didn't awaken the soul any more than being a glutton! I could never survive on a nut a day!"

"Well, if it was a big enough nut."

"You are still talking about actual nuts here and not male anatomy, right?"

Sheree pretended to vomit before saying, "Yes. I don't know. I come from a crazy Catholic family and honestly think most religion is bullshit."

"How can you say my religion is bullshit? I'm proud to be Buddhist despite my reluctance to believe everything verbatim!" Jennifer looked very pissed off, like a tiger whose meal just got taken by a vulture.

"I'm sorry!" Sheree said loudly. *Why do you always have to push things too far?*

Snickering, Jennifer said, "No, I'm just jacking with you."

Letting out a nervous laugh, "Sheree said, "Thank God, because for a second there I thought I'd offended you again. I should just watch what I say around people, because I have a tendency to just say what's on my mind. That or people can read my mind while I'm thinking bad thoughts about them."

"You're just expressionistic. I read your thoughts all the time just by looking at you. You're not telepathically projecting, if that's what you think," Jennifer informed her friend.

"Great. So, getting back to the whole religion thing, it's like this whole end of the world crap. I mean, it's 1999 and will soon be the year 2000. Predicting the end of the world based off of a new millennium is just stupid," Sheree continued.

"Well, doesn't the Bible say something about false prophets getting stoned?" Jennifer asked.

"Pretty sure these wack-jobs were stoned when they made their Y2K prophecies!" Sheree said with a wicked grin.

"A bit too much of the ganja, huh?" Jennifer added, nodding.

Doing her best impression, Sheree inhaled an imaginary joint and said, "Jesus, man, yeah I just saw him a mile back on Route 1. No, no, no, no man, he was like, invisible man. Yeah, it was like, dude, where are you man? And he's like all invisibly saying, I'm like right here dude! Hehehe… dude," then back in her normal voice, "And the fact that the guys who made it up will be the first to say they just got the date wrong because the actual millennial timeframe would be 2001 since there wasn't a Year Zero so be prepared and shit really irks my…"

"Can you please just drop it? Remember what you said about not saying what you think? I mean you're verbally projectile vomiting all over my new sweater!" Jennifer told her friend.

"That's so cute! Old Navy?" Sheree asked, copping a feel.

"Of course!" Jennifer responded.

"So are you going to tell me, or not?" Jennifer asked, trying to get it out of Sheree's mind like she'd been able to do so many times before.

Doing her best to remain unreadable, Sheree looked at her with one eye cocked open, a sly look on her face that made her look like a stroke victim. "You'll have to wait 'til Christmas."

Jennifer growled as she folded her arms. "You mean Buddhamas?"

"NO! I mean CHRISTMAS!!!" Sheree shouted, her voice echoing off the nearby trees and houses and possibly causing a few unstable snow piles to fall off.

Looking around to make sure nobody heard her friend, Jennifer said, "Okay, please calm down, I'm only joking, all right?"

"I know. C'mon. Let's go inside, it's freezing out here," Sheree insisted hugging herself to show that she was cold. "I just need to grab these last few bags out of my trunk and bring them in."

Noticing that all three bags were from Everything's A Dollar, Jennifer said, "Let me guess, my present is in one of those bags, isn't it?"

"No," Sheree lied. "I just bought some wrapping paper and gift bags there so I could spend more money on the gifts instead."

"Seems logical enough, Sheree. Got cocoa?" Jennifer asked.

"Of course!" Sheree said, closing the trunk. They went into the house and Sheree put the Everything's A Dollar bags next to the other bags and put on a kettle of water to boil for hot cocoa. "So, Jen, have you got your Christmas shopping done? I mean Buddhamas."

Jennifer looked at her with an unmistakably pathetic face. "Yeah right! I haven't even started yet!"

"Geez, and I thought that I was starting late!" Sheree said louder than she intended to, but then remembering that her and Jennifer were alone in the house so she didn't have to worry about her father telling her to keep it down so he could concentrate on the all important television program about some war she was too young to understand the importance of and she would understand when she was older and wiser and had children of her own.

"It's not like I have a massive amount of people to buy for. Let's see, I have to get something for you… yep, that's it," Jennifer told her, sitting down on one of the stools at the breakfast bar.

"I wish I only had one person to buy for! My family's huge! Sometimes I wish we were all Jehovah's Witnesses. Then I wouldn't have to worry about Christmas presents."

"Okay, now who's hypocritical?" Jennifer asked, head cocked on one shoulder with her jet-black hair perfectly framing her annoyed expression.

A whistle blew. The water was boiling, and the whistle was getting louder and louder, bursting through their conversation and overtaking the whole room. Steam shot out of the spout of the teapot creating a puffy cloud above it like a volcano's eruption. Jennifer placed her hands over her ears to cover them from the sound until Sheree took it off the stove and it grew quieter.

"Do you like yours really chocolaty or not?" Sheree asked as she scooped eight heaping teaspoons into her Sylvester the cat mug.

"Nah, just ten or eleven scoops is enough," Jennifer told her with a serious expression. "I don't want to be up all night!" she said all twitchy.

After having a laugh and having poured the hot water into the cups, Sheree asked, after sipping some of her frothy cocoa, "So, how are things with you and Chad?" Curiosity got the better of her since the whole "I have to get something for you… yep, that's it" convo.

"Since this afternoon, all right, I suppose," Jennifer told her in a way to remind her that they had already talked about that topic during lunch earlier that day, also taking a sip of her drink, savoring the thick white foamy whey floating on the top.

"Yeah, you sound a little uncertain?"

"Well, remember when I told you months ago that I thought he was gay or something?"

"Uh huh."

"I'm beginning to think he may just be asexual instead."

"Really?"

"Yeah."

"Why?"

"Oh, just that he never wants to make out unless it's a reenactment from a scene in a movie, you know, like it's all a game to him."

"Um, well, you both are only fourteen. And I'm almost positive that your little monkey still plays with cartoon action figures."

"Or dress up dolls!"

"Or manly-man action figures!"

"Because he's attracted to manly men!"

"Or wants to be one because he's such a lanky kid."

"Yeah, he is a bit lanky. Maybe I should let him go. It's just those make-out sessions of ours are so hot! He's a great kisser, really."

"So you still think he's asexual if he's making out with you, one of the hottest girls at Ravenwood High?"

"But it's just making out! It's like I'm just his beard. When am I going to see any action?"

"You're fourteen! Trust me okay, you want to wait on this one."

"I'm just afraid that he's one of those chronic masturbators, you know, the kind who only want to talk and cuddle and kiss then go home and jerk off all night. What's in it for me?"

"Again you freak, you're only fourteen. You can wait a while."

"Why? Have you ever, you know, done it?"

"That's beside the point."

"But if you're telling me to wait, I'd like to know why?"

"Because I don't think you are ready yet."

"Who are you to know when I am ready?"

"Your best friend who cares a ton of Death by Chocolate ice cream about you!"

"So you have, haven't you?"

"I'm not saying that I have or haven't, I'm just saying that you shouldn't be so eager to give up your virginity just for the sake of losing it. It should mean something, not just happen. You can't get it back once it's gone."

"Thank you, Dr. Sheree Hollins for that fantastic advice! Now if you'll please get off your high-horse and talk to me like an equal rather than a child, I'd very much appreciate it."

"I am two years older than you."

"But we're still in the same grade. Geez, get off my back."

"I'm sorry, just a touchy subject to me."

"And why is that, Dr. Sheree?"

"It just is, and don't call me doctor."

"Fine. Whatever."

"Okay, I'll tell you why. When I lived in Seattle, a friend of mine thought she was ready to have sex, and being the forward person she was, told her boyfriend she wanted to do it. So they were all ready for the big act and at the last minute she decided to back out. Apparently something clicked in her mind what she was about to do. Anyway, her boyfriend was all worked up and had made up his own mind he was going to have sex anyway and pinned her down, gagged her, and raped her. And, as if that wasn't bad enough, three of his buddies walked in on them and decided they wanted in on the action too and actually helped hold her down while they took turns screwing her."

"That couldn't happen with me because Chad doesn't have any friends, and besides, I could snap that boy in two if he ever tried anything like that, not that he would ever try anything like that. Chronic masturbator."

"Again, beside the point, and… he does so have friends! I saw him a half hour ago with like ten other cheerleaders at Pizza Schmizza!"

"So that was you, I thought so. He called my phone and told me he saw you but you just ignored him completely. I had to tell him that you probably didn't even notice him because you were too busy looking at your own reflection in the glass, you know, checking your hair out or something to make sure it wasn't out of place."

"Oh, thanks for making me conceited!"

"So now I made you conceited? I think you did that to yourself, honey!"

"Fine, I'm serious about our little sex talk though. It'll mean more if you wait till you are truly ready."

"Whatever you say, Mother."

"Jennifer!"

"Sorry, you just sound like my mom, going all after school special on my ass."

"Yeah, but my experience was real!"

"You mean your friend's," Jennifer corrected, suddenly suspicious Sheree was hiding something.

Realizing her mistake, Sheree responded, "That's what I meant."

Silence filled the room as they drank more of their hot cocoa, which had cooled down dramatically since their last sip, becoming lukewarm cocoa instead. Without realizing it, Sheree had chugged hers down to the undissolved bits at the bottom of the cup. "You want more?" she asked Jennifer, filling up the kettle with more water and putting it back on the burner to boil.

Looking at her watch, she saw that it was almost nine o'clock. "I really shouldn't," she told Sheree as she began scooping more of the chocolaty powder into her oversized mug.

"So, can you promise me that you'll wait?"

"Fine, it's not like the chronic masturbator and I are seriously going to get to third base anytime ever."

Cringing, Sheree asked, "Will you please stop calling Chad that?"

"What, chronic masturbator? That's what he is! Maybe I should join him and become a chronic masturbator too, and we can start a Masturbation Club at school or something cool like that where we meet and talk about techniques and tools, stuff of that sort you know," Jennifer informed Sheree in a rather excited voice. Mocking a Tammy Faye tear, she added, "It'll be beautiful."

"Good lord, you're weird."

"You have no idea."

"Yes I do."

"No you don't."

"Yeah, I think I do."

"Well, me and the C.M.A. don't think you do."

"The cee em ay?"

"Chronic Masturbators Association, silly!"

"Stop it with the chronic masturbator crap!" Sheree yelled as her family walked in the front door, arms loaded with bags of groceries from the market.

"What's this I hear about chronic masturbators?" her father asked with a mischievous grin plastered on his youthful face.

"Hi Mr. Hollins, we were just talking about a new club Sheree wants to form at school," Jennifer told him.

"You liar!" Sheree shouted, punching Jennifer's upper arm. "That was your idea, punk, fess up to it!"

Not wanting to miss out on the conversation, Brendon added, "Sheree, do you suffer from Chronic Masturbation Syndrome? If so, you're going to hell. Masturbators and fags all go to hell, that's what the Bible says. But not dykes because God likes girl-on-girl action as much as the next straight man!"

"Brendon!" Mrs. Hollins shouted, her husband in the background laughing. "Where did you learn to talk like that?"

Rolling his eyes as if the answer was obvious, he said, "School of course."

"But you don't really believe that, do you?" Mr. Hollins asked his son, the shock-laughter wearing off.

"No, I tell all those right-wingers on the playground that they should learn the original Hebrew and Greek that the Bible was written in and the grammar from those eras as well in order to fully understand that you can't accurately quote the Bible in English because too much gets lost in translation," Brendon told everyone, shocking them all.

"Okay, I'm a little freaked out. Where did you learn that?" Mrs. Hollins questioned, knowing for certain it wasn't from their household as they had pretty much banned most religious talk since parting from the church all those years ago.

With a smile, Brendon told her, "From Johnny's dads of course. They are part of the Gays for Jesus group that meets every Tuesday down at the community center! I've been to a couple meetings with them."

A concerned look was on his mom and dad's faces; Sheree and Jennifer on the other hand were giggling. "Johnny and I play basketball in the gym with all the other kids."

"I had no idea that there were that many gay people in Ravenwood, that's all," his mother told him. "And Johnny has two dads?"

Nodding his head, Brendon asked, "Really Mom, you honestly didn't know that? That and the fact that we live right next door to a pair of lovely lesbians named Lucy and Charlene who just happen to be raising four girls and a boy while there is no man in sight?"

"Even I knew that," Mr. Hollins grunted.

Mrs. Hollins still looked clueless. "I thought they were just... friends."

"They are special friends. Ah, what it was like to be so ignorant. I miss that. Good times," Brendon said, looking at some invisible person.

Still in shock, their mother said, "It just seems that you're awfully young to know so much… um… adult stuff, like, uh, masturbation."

"Oh please, Mom. I mean masturbation is so fourth grade."

"Brendon, you are in the fourth grade," Sheree reminded her brother.

"I know, that's why I like to sing…" he said, clearing his throat then singing, "…masturbation, super masturbation, masturbation, a game we like to play!"

Cringing like her daughter did earlier at all the masturbation talk, Mrs. Hollins suggested, "Can we just not talk about masturbation, it just seems so… wrong."

"It's perfectly natural, honey," Mr. Hollins told his wife. "Besides, all this talk of lesbians and masturbation is making me horny."

"Eeeauuw!" Sheree and Brendon and Jennifer screeched simultaneously, clenching their eyes as shut as they could.

"You've got a sick mind Frank, in front of the children no less," Mrs. Hollins said sternly, but with an afterthought of a smile on her face.

"And that's what you love most about me, Beth!" Mr. Hollins returned, grinning from ear to ear.

They stared at each other for a second, then, as they were running up the stairs, they shouted, "Brendon, Sheree, put the groceries away!" before their bedroom door slammed shut.

"Okay, I think that was the most disturbing conversation this family has ever had," Sheree commented, taking the kettle off the stove just as it started to whistle that it was ready. "Even the water's all hot and bothered!"

"Good one, Sheree!" Brendon said, raising his hand in a high-five position, which Sheree gladly slapped.

"Damn, Sheree, you da' man!" Jennifer said, doing her best Ebonics but sounding more like an Asian girl with a noticeable accent.

Filling up their mugs with the hot water, Sheree accepted her congratulations. "Hey Brendon, I'll give you two dollars if you put all the groceries away?"

"Okay!" he told her. "I was just going to do it anyway because you've got company, but if you're going to pay me, hey, I'll take it!"

Glaring at her little brother, she muttered, "Punk ass."

"Mmm…" Jennifer let out after taking the first drink of her second cup of cocoa. "Can you believe you're parents are up there right now, just above our heads having sex?"

Somewhat disgusted, Sheree told her friend, "Please don't put images into my head that I'll have to claw my eyeballs out to rid my mind of. I like my eyes, thank you very much, and I'd like to keep them if you don't mind."

"Yeah, I wonder what sex is like," Brendon said out of the blue as he put the eggs in the fridge just under the meat and cheese drawer.

"You'll find out when you're NEVER!" Sheree told him with wide eyes.

Agreeing, Brendon said back, "You're right. Girls are icky. I think I'll just be a chronic masturbator like you two."

"Are you even old enough to…" Jennifer started but was interrupted by Brendon.

"My friend Tommy Gufflebacht said he's got pubes, and I'm starting to get hair under my armpits and…"

"That turned out to be mold," Sheree reminded her little brother.

"Yeah, but it looked like hair, didn't it?" he asked.

"Uh huh, hairy mold," she said matter-of-factly.

"Whatever, Sheree, boys are different from girls. We have different parts. You don't know anything about us men," Brendon said with a stuck-up tone in his voice.

Jennifer and Sheree, laughing at his last comment, both said, "Okay Brendy, you're a man all right!" They stared at each other in disbelief that they'd say the same exact thing at the same exact time and concurrently said, "Jinx!" Then, as if their brains were in complete tune with each other, also said, "Oh that is too weird."

"Stop the insanity!" Brendon shouted, hoping it would break his sister and her friend's psychic connection to one another.

It seemed to have worked, as Sheree and Jennifer began talking about school and how they couldn't wait until three o'clock tomorrow when their winter vacation officially started. The kitchen floor quickly piled with empty plastic bags as Brendon continued to put what seemed like enough food for an army in the pantry and refrigerator, sans his usual interjections. However, once their hot cocoa was gone again, so seemed to be their conversation as well.

"I should get going," Jennifer told Sheree, stepping over and around the piles of blue bags on the floor to rinse out her mug in the sink.

Getting up off her stool, Sheree said, "I'll give you a ride home," doing the same, leaving her mug on the counter and telling Jennifer to leave hers there too.

"Thanks. Goodnight Brendon! Don't fall out of any trees!" Jennifer called out maliciously as she headed toward the front door.

As if it started hurting again, Brendon began rubbing his recently healed arm, glaring at her and thinking of something horrible to say, but could only come up with blowing a raspberry.

"I'll be back in a minute Bren. Thanks again for putting the food away, I owe you one," Sheree told her brother.

"Actually," Brendon said, "You owe me two, as in, two dollars."

Smiling, Sheree informed her brother, "Actually," mimicking him, "If you would have paid attention, I had my fingers crossed when I offered it."

"I knew I should have never trusted the Whore of Babylon!" Brendon shouted to his sister and making a dramatically good Charlton Heston pose.

Perplexed, Sheree finally had to ask, "Okay, so when did you get all biblical?"

"School, well, during recess that is."

"You really are just weird like Mom said about you."

"Yeah, I'm going to be a televangelist when I grow up. You know how much dinero those guys make?!"

"Uh huh, because they're scam artists."

"Yes, but they're scam artists in the name of our Lord and Savior Jesus Christ! There's got to be something to be said about that!"

"I believe they call it something like twenty years to life, and after that it's called hell!"

"You don't have to be so negative all the time, chronic masturbator," Brendon pouted, folding his arms across his chest. He genuinely looked hurt.

"That's right, Brendon. Just don't go looking in my underwear drawer because you might find Mr. Pinkie," Sheree told him.

"Huh? Who's Mr. Pinkie? And when did Mom call me weird?" Brendon asked with confusion.

But Sheree just gave him a smile and went out the door, meeting up with Jennifer who was already at the car's passenger door waiting to get in. "You just missed a classic chat I had with Brendon where I told him not to go looking for my dildo," she said as she unlocked the passenger side door.

"You've got a dildo?" Jennifer asked, opening the door and waiting for Sheree to unlock her side before seating herself.

"No, but he doesn't know that," she told her, sitting down in the driver's seat, Jennifer sitting as well, both closing their doors as Sheree started the car.

"Darn, I was going to ask to borrow it!"

"Free at last!" Sheree shouted to the world as she opened the entrance doors of Ravenwood High School, the three o'clock bell having rung only moments before. As she walked toward her little blue sedan, she waved bye and said, "Merry Christmas," to just about everyone she saw. "Hey, Jennifer," she yelled when she saw her friend come around the school from the side. "Have a Merry Christmas!"

Jennifer ignored her.

Walking closer and closer to Sheree, Jennifer was wearing an evil grin.

"Jennifer?"

She came closer. Close enough so that Sheree could see that she was hiding something behind her back.

"Watch out, Sheree, I'm comin' to get ya'," Jennifer said loudly with a frightening voice.

What does she have behind her back? Why is she coming closer to me? Why does she continue to stare at me with fiery eyes? Stop being paranoid, Sheree!

Jennifer was getting even closer to her, only a few yards away now.

Why can't I move? She must have me under some kind of spell. Wait, Jennifer doesn't know magic, right? Noooooooo! This can't be happening.

"I'm gonna getchya, Sheree," Jennifer repeated.

She's got a knife or a gun or some weapon hiding behind her. She's going to kill me! But why? She's my friend! Why can't I move? We've gotten so close the last few weeks. I can't believe that she's the one who's been terrorizing me. I can't!

But there was Jennifer, maliciously concealing her weapon, waiting to unleash it upon her best friend, and Sheree looked helpless and afraid.

Sheree felt like she was having an asthma attack. Her breaths becoming rapid and short, getting harder and harder to breathe. The thin winter air began getting heavy, too heavy to breathe in.

Heavier.

Heavier.

Heavier and heavier until she stopped breathing all together.

Her frightened body could not move.

There are so many people around us. Don't any of them see her? Can't they see what's happening? Why aren't they trying to stop her? And why can't I talk?

Jennifer was so close to Sheree now that she could reach out and touch her if only her body was able to do so. If only it wasn't frozen to the snow covered ground. If only she hadn't become a statue the very moment she needed to run.

Why does she want to kill me?

Jennifer's arm moved out from behind her back.

"NOOOOOOOOOOOOOOOO!"

Chapter 12
Merry Christmas, Sheree

Jennifer grinned wide, showing her bright white, perfectly straight teeth.

"I gotcha!"

"Nooooooo!" Sheree screamed again, closing her eyes.

Suddenly she felt a cold blow to her face.

Freezing.

Stinging.

Did she just shoot me? Is this what it feels like to be shot? Sheree wondered, fearing what she would find when she opened her eyes, but realizing that she had to know what happened and why she felt all cold and wet on her cheek. The moment of truth; she opened her eyes, expecting to see blood pouring out all over herself, but instead found a pile of freezing white powder slide from her face and onto her coat and shoes.

Snow?

There was laughter all around her, and she saw Jennifer, tumbled over on the ground laughing hysterically like it was the funniest thing in the world. Other students in the parking lot were pointing and laughing as well as they walked by. After Sheree wiped the snow off her face, she scooped up a ball from the snow-covered ground, hoping it was embedded with some gravel or bird poop or anything foreign. Aiming toward Jennifer, she threw the ball into the air, landing on her friend's head.

"Take that you bitch!" Sheree told her best friend, jumping up in the air with excitement from the hit.

Taking advantage of Sheree's victory dance, Jennifer grabbed her by the ankles and yanked her down to the ground. Caught off guard, Sheree landed on her butt and screamed, "That's going to bruise!" as she caressed it. The two continued to throw snow at each other until their bare hands were numb from the cold. They sat in the snow, wondering what they were going to do with themselves as students swerved around them as they left the premises.

"So, Jen, how are things with Chad and you?" Sheree finally asked, wiping her frozen hands off onto her blue jeans and rubbing them together to warm them back up.

Jennifer stared at her shoes, realizing that she probably just ruined them from playing in the snow and rolling her eyes at the question. "Good lord woman, we talked about this last night and at lunch too!"

"I know, but things can change in three hours," Sheree said, feeling her bottom go from just being cold to wet and cold.

"Oh, I just broke up with him," Jennifer said matter-of-factly.

"You what?! Why did you do that? You two got along great!"

"He just got, boring, you know."

"Since lunch when you were talking again about how great of a kisser he is and…"

"And how he only wants to make out to love scenes from musicals! It's for the best. The boy is gay, even if he doesn't know it yet!"

"Uh huh, so you dumped him because you were bored with him and he might be gay? I guess that's a legitimate reason."

"It is!"

"How'd he take it?"

"Heartbroken as hell, I really didn't think it was going to be that big of a deal. I mean, after all he is only fourteen."

"Like you."

Jennifer stuck out her tongue, deciding to get up off the snow and out of the way of the cars that seemed to be getting annoyed with their choice of location to sit and chat, almost all of them honking their horns and the people inside them yelling obscenities and making gestures with their middle fingers.

Doing the same, Sheree brushed off any snow that hadn't melted and seeped into her clothing, returning the birdie to who she thought was a student, but realized it was a teacher when she got a closer look. "Sorry!" she yelled out to Mrs. O'Hurley as she drove by, hoping her favorite teacher could hear her apology. They continued to talk as they walked toward her car.

"I mean, boys don't take this stuff that seriously, do they?" Jennifer asked, suddenly wondering if she should have been a little more thoughtful.

"That depends, how'd you break up with him?" Sheree asked, brushing the small amount of snow that had fallen during the school hours off her little blue sedan's windshield.

"I was just like, 'Hey Chad! I'm breaking up with you! Have a great vacation!' Should I have maybe written it in a letter?" Jennifer wondered.

"You did not say it like that, did you?"

"Yeah I did, Sheree. Oh, but he is such a great kisser! Great, now I'm having second thoughts. Thanks. It's all your fault, you know. Shit. You've gone and made me think about it now. I hate you."

A pleased expression formed on Sheree's face as she looked at her dismayed friend who had a scowl on hers. "I suppose you want me to give you a ride home though, right?"

"If it isn't too much trouble, after all, what are friends who can drive for if not to give their non-driving friends a lift?"

"Get in."

Once in the car and halfway out of the parking lot, Sheree was going to tell Jennifer that she thought she was hiding a gun behind her back and not a snowball, but decided that was a bad idea. *She already thinks I'm crazy, I don't know if I want to add paranoid to my résumé!* Instead, she asked Jennifer if she wanted to go with her to the outlet center to pick up a few more presents. There were only two people to cross off her shopping list and she mostly had to get stuff for her brother.

"You know Sheree," Jennifer responded with a sigh, "I'd love to, and you know how much it pains me to turn down a shopping trip, but my dad's coming into town tonight and Mommy Dearest wants me to help her clean the house and help her make dinner and doll ourselves up so daddy can pat us on our head and give us money until he comes back next month."

"That bites," Sheree said, shaking her head as she turned onto Main Street from the school's parking lot. "At least you're an only child otherwise you'd probably have even more to do!"

"Are you kidding?!" Jennifer screamed, throwing her hands into the air and hitting the ceiling of the car, causing her to stare at it as if she was wondering when that got there. "If I had brothers and sisters I'd make them do all my dirty work. They'd be my minions!"

Laughing, Sheree told her, "Trust me, it doesn't work that way. They're nothing but big pains in the ass if you want my opinion."

Rolling her eyes in disbelief, Jennifer asked, "So you don't think Brendon would do anything you asked him to without even giving it a second thought?"

"Are you kidding?!" Sheree screamed, throwing her hands into the air and hitting the ceiling of the car and then, realizing that she was the driver, quickly put her hands back onto the steering wheel just in time to make the turn onto Jennifer's street.

"Yes, you're right, Brendon's a punk."

"Ass. You forgot the ass part. It's okay, my mom does it all the time."

"Sorry."

It seemed that their conversation ended perfectly as Sheree pulled into the Hoang's driveway. "I'll call you when I'm done shopping. We need to get together before Christmas."

"Buddhamas," Jennifer corrected her.

"CHRISTMAS!!!" Sheree exclaimed back.

Smiling one of her mood enhancing smiles she was famous for, Jennifer waved goodbye to Sheree as she walked up to the door and into her house. Slightly disappointed that Jennifer couldn't come with her, but not entirely as this would give her a chance to find more gifts for her as well, being that she was the other name on her shopping list, she pulled out of the Hoang's driveway and headed back to Main Street. Next stop: the mall, or better known as the Ravenwood Factory Outlet Shopping Center. But this time she was skipping the dollar store.

It only took her half an hour to find a couple more gifts for Jennifer and that perfect present for her brother; a Super Samurai Slug action figure with special oozing trail feature. "He's going to love this!" she thought out loud as she had it rung up at the discount toy store, picking up an extra container of ooze. "Oh cool, it comes with a free comic book too?" she asked the clerk, who looked like he was going to strangle the next person who asked that question while at the same time looking oddly familiar.

"Yes. Everybody gets a free limited edition Super Samurai Slugs comic book with purchase, or without purchase, or just for the hell of it. You hear that everyone? Free comic books!" he shouted to the rest of the people in line, picking up a pile of the comics and throwing them in every direction.

"You want your comic book? Here! Take it! Take your fucking comic book then! TAKE THEM ALL!!!"

Deciding that it was time to make her escape, and realizing that she would never work in retail ever thanks to that demonstration of a loss in sanity, she left the store, watching people covering their heads and faces to shield them from the onslaught of free slug comic books. Walking back to her car, she wondered if the clerk was going to be fired or just quit his job when she heard from behind her some guy yell, "I'm free! Free at last, free at last! Thank God Almighty, I'm free at last!"

It was the clerk. And she suddenly realized who it was.

"Ryan, is that you?"

Looking down at his name badge, he said, "It appears so. That's what this says anyway," as he tore it from his shirt, tossing it into a nearby receptacle. "So, what's your name hot stuff?"

"Sheree? Sheree Hollins? Your sister Angela's best friend for like years?" she questioningly told him, his head shaking 'not-a-clue' until the last one.

"Oh! Sheree, right!" he said, slapping his forehead. "Wow, you got really hot."

Not sure what to say, she said, "Uh, thanks. You didn't… say you were going to be in Ravenwood. I thought you were going to U Dub?"

"Dropped out, college sucks. I've decided to make it big time in the real world…"

"Of retail? Yeah, it's working out great for you," Sheree finished.

Nodding like he was a bobblehead, he asked, "So, you're like sixteen now, aren't you?"

"Yeah," Sheree told him, feeling really uncomfortable.

"So, that's like legal age of consent, if you know what I mean," he said with the same bobbleheadedness.

"I suppose. Of course, my husband might not agree. You see, he's a big guy, three hundred pound football player for Wazzu, and he's very possessive of me. Doesn't like it when other people show any sign of interest in me," Sheree lied.

"Whoah! You're married? Damn, sorry, I, uh, didn't mean anything by…"

"Listen, Ryan, I gotta go before my husband gets worried about me and thinks I'm with some crazy college dropout!"

"No, go, please! Bye!" he shouted, running through the parking lot and getting into his old beat up pickup truck.

"Whew," Sheree sighed. "I can't believe I used to have a crush on that guy, blehck!" she said as she unlocked her little blue sedan's door, tossing her bags onto the passenger's seat before getting in. "What was I thinking?"

Driving home, she contemplated her middle school choices in men, all the while a really annoying Christmas song was playing on the radio. You know, the kind that once they get in your head, they never want to leave. Always there, playing themselves over and over until it drives you insane. And it's never the whole song either, just the chorus or some other repetitive portion of it. And now, it was stuck in Sheree's head.

"Feliz Navidad!" Sheree sang as she was wrapping the last of her Christmas presents. "Damn it! Why won't that song get out of my head? Curse you Christmas music and all your irritatingness!"

It was the day before Christmas. Christmas Eve. And two days since Sheree had even heard the song that had managed to lodge itself into repeat mode in her brain. Tossing the dollar store earrings that she bought for Jennifer, along with a couple other things she got for her into a metallic gift bag, she looked at her watch, noticing it was time to leave. She scribbled something on a note card, put it on top of the bag and brought it down the creaking stairs with her.

"Dad, I'm going to Jennifer's to take her present to… what the hell? Are you reading?" Sheree asked, a shocked look on her face.

Mr. Hollins looked up from the newspaper. "Yes."

"But the television isn't broken, what's going on? Where's my father and what have you done with him?" Sheree interrogated, pointing her finger in his direction.

"Ha ha, very funny little girl. Just be back before dinner, okay?" her dad told her.

"I will. See ya later," she said, opening the hall closet and taking out her blue down coat, sliding it on.

"Tell Jen hi for me," he said, picking the newspaper back up and searching for the article he was reading before Sheree interrupted his train of thought.

When she opened the old front door, a gust of cold air flew into the house, nearly knocking her over. She closed the door behind her and ran to her little blue sedan parked on the street.

"Brrrr! it's chilly out here tonight," she said, hugging herself.

After brushing off some of the snow from the windshield with the sleeve of her coat, she unlocked the door to get in, quickly putting the key into the ignition and starting the car, letting it warm up for a few seconds before she took off. When she turned the headlights on, they darted directly at the Ravenwood Cemetery, illuminating the cast iron fence and headstones encased inside it. After making a U-Turn in the middle of the street she headed for Jennifer's house.

"Feliz Navidad!" she sang again. "Aaaah! Make it stop, please make it stop!" she cried.

As soon as she turned onto Baker Street, the street that Jennifer lived on, she noticed that almost every house was brightly decorated with lights and other Christmas ornaments, something she didn't notice when she dropped Jennifer off at home a couple days ago. It was rare to see anything like that on Song's End. All the houses were so dark and gloomy all the time. Even during Christmas. Only one of the houses had lights: theirs. Along with their life size Nativity scene and about fifty Santas, Frostys, Rudolphs and dozens of other Christmastime characters. The rest were still old and nightmarish looking.

It was easy to spot the Hoang residence amongst all the Christmassy displays, as it was the only one without. When she pulled into Jennifer's driveway, she saw Jennifer in the front yard making a snowman. Probably so it would look like they had some Christmas cheer, even if they didn't celebrate.

"Sheree!" Jennifer squealed as she stepped in front of the torso she had just put in place. "You're ruining my snow!"

Looking down through the open driver's side door, she told her friend, "There isn't even any snow on this side," as she stepped out of the vehicle.

"I was just kidding. I already used that part. Can't have a snowman built from yard snow, you know? Just gets all grassy and muddy and then you've got no scenery in which a snowman should fit into," Jennifer told Sheree as if she was an expert on the fine art of snow sculptures.

"Unless you were going for the Pigpen look," Sheree informed her friend as she reached over to the passenger side to get the gift bag.

"*Charlie Brown Christmas*, I love that show!" Jennifer said nostalgically. "We should go watch it now."

Sheree slammed the door to her car and rushed over to her friend, careful not to destroy Jennifer's precious snow. "But you've only got half a snow man built? What will the neighbors think?"

"They probably think that we're Buddhist and don't celebrate Christmas, because that's what my mother has been telling every single one of them for the last three weeks, cursing them all high electric bills!" Jennifer said rather loudly. "How embarrassing, I mean, can't we just be like everyone else and decorate for Jesus? It's what He would have wanted."

"I've got the opposite on my street."

"That's because it's haunted. Lighting it would probably scare off the ghosts!"

"Well our house is lit like the Griswold's and my ghost is still there!"

"Oh, *National Lampoon's Christmas Vacation*! I love that movie too! We should watch that instead."

"Only got time for Snoopy."

"Oh all right. Fine. Be that way."

Sheree put her hand out, showing off the shiny bag full of Jennifer's presents.

"For me?" Jennifer asked, looking at the gift bag Sheree had in her hand.

"Uh, yeah," Sheree said, handing the bag over to Jennifer.

"Ooh, it's so shiny. C'mon, let's go inside," Jennifer said, taking Sheree by the arm and tugging her into the house where there was still absolutely no sign of Christmas. However, Sheree did spot a fat Buddha on the fireplace hearth with a bowl of fruit in front of it. "Feed the Buddha, brings good luck," she told Sheree, answering the question her friend never asked. Jennifer pulled the tissue paper that Sheree put into the bag to hide the gifts and tossed it on the blue carpet, the note card falling to the ground. "Ooooooh! Thank you, Sheree!" Jennifer ran over to her and gave her a hug. "I love them!" she declared, putting them close to her ear and looking at her reflection in the mirror by the door to see how they looked on her.

"You're welcome, Jen. So did you get me anything?" Sheree asked excitedly in return, picking up the card and returning it to Jennifer.

"Nope," Jennifer said flatly, opening the card to read it. "Oh, how sweet!"

What?! I spent my hard-earned money on her and she didn't get me anything in return? What a slimeball! Sheree was furious. Unable to control her anger any longer, she was about to go ballistic.

"Kidding! Here you go, Sheree," Jennifer said as she handed Sheree a box. It was wrapped in a floral Christmas design.

"Thanks!" Sheree squealed with delight, holding the box with both hands and admiring its beauty.

"Hurry up, open it," Jennifer insisted.

As Sheree carefully unwrapped the paper on the outside of the heavy box, she could tell Jennifer was becoming impatient, but she didn't care. The paper was so pretty and she didn't want to rip any of it. Finally when she was finished taking the wrapping paper off, she pried off the lid of the box, and gasped.

Chapter 13
Another Gift from Another Grave

"You like?" Jennifer inquired, her eyes wide and awaiting an answer.

Nearly in shock, Sheree continued to stare inside the open box, not believing her eyes. *She bought me a sweater? This looks so expensive!* Sheree thought as she examined the royal purple knitted sweater. Guilt began surging through her as she thought about the gift she bought Jennifer. She gave her such a cheap present, and Jennifer went out and bought her what looked like a fifty-dollar sweater. "Thanks! I love it!" Sheree shouted, pulling it out from the box and letting the paper she had so carefully taken off slip to the ground as well, the corner of the box puncturing it as it fell too. Walking over to Jennifer, she gave her a hug, the surprise from the gift almost unbearable.

"Do you really like it? I wasn't sure if you even liked purple," Jennifer asked with a questioning look on her bright face.

"Yes, I really do. Purple is my favorite color!" Sheree stated.

Or at least it is now.

"Thank God, because I was afraid you'd hate it and I can't take it back," Jennifer told her.

"Oh my gawd, Jen, this looks so expensive, and it's so soft!" Sheree said, rubbing the material with her fingers.

A mischievous smile formed on Jennifer's face before she said, "Looks can be deceiving, Sheree. You probably spent more on my present than I spent on yours."

"Somehow I doubt that," Sheree told her, examining the sweater and holding it up to her body.

"Three bucks on clearance. Had a hole in it, but I fixed it and you'll never figure out where it was. You?"

"Dollar store earrings."

Widening her eyes to the point that they looked like they were going to pop out of their sockets, Jennifer yelled, "No way! You got those great earrings from a dollar store?"

"Everything's A Dollar. And the kitty T-shirt and matching bracelet from Claire's... on clearance for a buck each," Sheree told Jennifer, shocked that they were discussing the one thing that was taboo when it came to Christmas presents.

"Cool, so we both spent the same amount on each other!" Jennifer said jumping up and down, rattling the glass on the coffee table next to her.

"Yeah, cool, we're both cheapskates!" Sheree said, mimicking Jennifer's excitedness.

Nodding her head like Bobble-head Ryan, Jennifer told her, "Yes, but cheap with style."

"You got company?" a voice said from around the corner.

It was Jennifer's mom, who was about the same height as Jennifer, but rounder in all locations.

Putting her hand over her face, Jennifer said as she let it slide down, "Mom, this is Sheree. Remember, my friend I'm always talking about. The one you took home that one time."

"Ohhhhhhh, the crazy one who see invisible spider!" Mrs. Hoang said with a thick Vietnamese accent, wearing wide eyes and a wicked smile. "Yes, I know her."

Turning her head away from Mrs. Hoang and toward Jennifer, Sheree asked, "You told you're mother about my hallucinations?"

"Well, yeah," Jennifer told her, shrugging her shoulders as if it was no big deal.

Reaching over and petting Sheree's head, Mrs. Hoang told her, "You have pretty golden hair. I like it." Then, pulling her hand away and grabbing her purse from the coffee table she said, "I pay you twenty dollar for it."

"Oh my gawd," Jennifer said rolling her eyes.

"What does she mean?" Sheree asked, confused.

"My mother wants your hair," Jennifer informed her friend.

"Oh!" Sheree said, turning to Mrs. Hoang, "It's Clairol number..."

"I don't think you understand," Jennifer began to tell her. "She wants *your* hair."

"Huh?" a clueless Sheree said, still not comprehending.

"Mom wants to have your hair cut off and made into a wig for herself," Jennifer told her, making her mother's intentions clear as a bell for her friend.

"Yes, yes, twenty dollar!" Mrs. Hoang offered again excitedly, practically shoving the bill down Sheree's throat.

"What?! No! NO! I like my hair!" she said, protecting it with both hands and the purple sweater. "It's mine!"

Laughing, Jennifer assured Sheree, "It's okay, I'll make sure that she knows it's not for sale," turning toward her mom to say in Vietnamese, "Tóc của cô là không phải để bán, nên ngừng làm phiền cô, được không?!"

"Con gái!" Mrs. Hoang shouted.

"Mẹ!" Jennifer shouted back.

Shaking her head and putting her money back into the wallet from her purse, Mrs. Hoang told Sheree, "Too bad. No one else offer you twenty dollar for that dung heap. You should take my offer while still good. I pay you," and she kept talking as she walked back into the hallway and to her bedroom, ending in Vietnamese curses to which Jennifer's eyes went wide with astonishment, never having heard them come out of her mother before.

"Well Sheree, now you've met my crazy mother," Jennifer said embarrassingly.

"Um, yay?" Sheree said back, not sure how to respond to someone wanting to buy the hair right off her head. And for such a low asking price too! "So where's your dad? Didn't you say he was in town?"

"I don't know," Jennifer shrugged. "He might still be. Maybe he's at the bar, or China, or at the foot massage place getting a hand job."

"Um, yay?" Sheree repeated, not sure how to respond to that last possibility her friend suggested.

"Seriously, I have no idea. He says he'll be in town for a week, and after a couple hours just takes off again without saying a word. I really don't know what he does with his time," Jennifer said, sounding a little hurt before beaming another smile. "Snoopy time!"

After watching *A Charlie Brown Christmas*, Sheree said goodbye to Jennifer, thanking her again for the sweater and apologizing that she couldn't stay longer. Her parents were having a Christmas Eve dinner, and her grandparents were going to be there. And while they were all going to see each other the next day, her father insisted on having his mom and dad over for dinner, but refused to let them stay in the house.

"That woman is crazy!" he proclaimed as Sheree walked through the door. "Do you really want my mother staying with us, Beth?"

Agreeing it was for the better good of all their sanities, Mrs. Hollins called the Ravenwood Inn to make sure the reservations they had made last week were still confirmed. "Hi honey," she said to Sheree who was putting her coat in the closet. "Yes, I'd like to confirm reservations for Hollins please."

"Hollins. Yes. They just checked in about ten minutes ago? Oh good, thank you very much," her mother said, hanging up the phone. "They're here! Did you have fun at Jennifer's?"

"Loads. Her mother tried to buy my hair for twenty dollars, can you believe that?" Sheree told her mom who nonchalantly nodded. Taking out the purple sweater from its box, she held it up. "Isn't this gorgeous?"

"Ooh, I like it. Chenille?" her mother asked, feeling the softness of the knitted sweater with both of her hands.

Nodding her head, Sheree said back, scrunching her nose, "Yeah it is, don't you just love it?"

"Well if it's missing, you'll know who took it!" her dad said, looking over at the two of them admiring the purple sweater.

"Oh hell no, you're not all Ed Wood, are you Dad?" Sheree asked sarcastically.

Hands on his hips, he said overdramatically, "Sans the angora, my weakness is chenille."

"Yeah, Uncle Billy told me all about you, Dad," Brendon said from the family room, taking his eyes off the video game he was playing.

"Oh please," Mr. Hollins said, rolling his eyes. "Like Billy has room to talk, I've seen his closet and it looks more like your mother's than mine!"

Defending his favorite uncle, Brendon said, "That's because he's a transvestite!"

"No, he's a drag queen."

"No he's not."

"Brendon, he is. A transvestite is a person who dresses like the opposite sex and lives that gender. A drag queen on the other hand, is a gay man who wears women's clothes for performances," he informed his son.

Seeing that this conversation was not going to include her, Mrs. Hollins went back into the kitchen to check on how dinner was coming along. Wanting to see how it panned out, Sheree stayed put.

"No way!" Brendon said loudly, his eyes wide open.

"Way!" their dad said, mimicking his son.

Laughing quietly, Sheree sat on the sofa's arm in the living room. "Ah, what it was like to be so ignorant. Good times. Seriously Brendon, didn't you even stop to wonder why Uncle Billy has lived with Uncle Jack since, like, before you were even born?"

"I thought they were both dad's brothers," he said innocently. "You mean, Uncle Jack isn't even related to me?"

Shaking his head no, Mr. Hollins said, "No, Jack is your Uncle Billy's husband.

"Well," Brendon said, straightening up, "I guess that explains why they are my godfathers, and I have no godmother. Huh, go figure. Oh well!" he said, shrugging his shoulders and running back to the family room to resume his video game when the doorbell rang.

"Merry Christmas!" Grandma and Grandpa Hollins shouted in unison as Sheree opened the large front door, both of their sets of arms outstretched for hugs and Grandma's hair still in curlers that have probably been in since the 1970s.

"The itsy bitsy spider went up the water spout…"

Far too excited about the next day to fall asleep, Sheree was already awake when the small voice began for its last time.

"Down came the snow and closed the spider out…"

"Huh? It's frozen now?" she said in a frightened confusion, nearly laughing at the absurd image of a spider completely encased in an ice cube that had entered her mind.

"The sun rose nice and hot and set the spider free...

...Oh poor, poor Jennifer, it really was a scream!"

"Oh no! It got Jennifer!" Sheree shrieked, quickly grabbing her phone to dial Jennifer's number.

One ring.

Two rings.

Growing impatient, she couldn't stand listening to the ringing, the never ending ringing. Sheree had to know if her friend was alive. And for some reason the ice cube spider wouldn't leave her imagination alone, and now it had taken on a personality all its own, complete with a black top hat and a French chef knife with blood dripping from the tip of it, and wearing a wide toothless grin like the Grinch.

Please pick up the phone. Please pick up the phone. Oh, Jennifer, be all right. Please!

"Hello?" a tired voice answered.

"Whew," Sheree sighed in relief.

"Helloooo?"

"Oh, Merry Christmas, Jen!"

"Not again. You heard the voice, didn't you Sheree?" Jennifer inquired with a hint of annoyance in the background of her voice.

"Well..." Sheree started to say, trying to come up with a better excuse.

"Please. Why else would you call me at four o' clock in the morning?" Jennifer asked, sitting up in her bed and angrily realizing that she wasn't going to be able to get back to sleep.

"I'm telling you, it's real. I know that it has something to do with all these accidents that have happened. Remember Jennifer? I told you that you're the next victim. The voice said that it was after you," Sheree reminded her friend, fiddling with the spiral telephone cord.

"Okay Sheree, first of all that was, what, three months ago. Has anything happened to me yet? No. Not one thing. I think that this is all in your imagination. You're just letting it get to you, that's all."

"Jennifer, you know that this thing, whatever it is, is real. You heard it for yourself in my room that night you stayed over," Sheree said, trying her best to make her friend understand the danger that she was in.

"No I didn't. I just said that to make you feel better," Jennifer revealed.

Could this be true? Could Jennifer really have just told Sheree that she heard the voice to relieve her conscious? But Brendon, he's heard it too, right? Or was that whole incident in her head as well? Everything was becoming so confusing to Sheree and she was unable to remember which memories were real and which were made up, and screaming incessantly in her head for a reason as to why the damned knife-wielding, top hat wearing, now dancing spider was still in her head when she needed to concentrate on saving her friend.

"This can't be happening," Sheree said quietly.

"It's true. I didn't hear anything," she told Sheree again.

"But, but, then why did you want to go down to the basement?"

"I was just curious what was in there, I guess. I don't know… it's too early in the morning to be talking. I can't think straight."

Why would she lie to me?

"The only real part about that night was that weirdo that broke into the house and knocked us both out," Jennifer told Sheree. "They never caught him, did they?"

That night.

The blow to her head left Sheree in a coma for a week. When she woke up, she was convinced that it had to be Jennifer who hit her over the head, but why? It couldn't be Jennifer, could it? Throughout all of what had happened in the last few months, Jennifer was her confidant, her best friend. How could it possibly be her? Then again, she did leave Sheree's hospital room with those evil words, "Don't tell anyone about our little secret, or something bad might happen." The words brought back all of her fear that she felt when she was in the basement alone with her.

The bugs.

The darkness.

The terror.

"Sheree, helloooow? Are you still there?" Jennifer asked.

Blinking out of her thoughts, Sheree told her, "Yeah, I'm still here. Why, were you hoping that I was dead or something?"

"What do you mean by that?" Jennifer asked loudly, shocked by the accusation.

Refusing to answer the question, Sheree said, "I hope that this thing… this ghost comes after you and does what it says it will do!" She knew that she was starting to sound like a crazy person, but she didn't care, she was too angry to care what she said.

"Fine! And a Merry Christmas to you too, bitch!" Jennifer shouted back, slamming her phone down.

The dial tone could be heard from Sheree's receiver. Doing the same, she threw her phone down onto the base, but so hard it knocked it off her bedside table, landing on the hardwood floor and causing it to make a faint ringing sound.

"Grrrrrrrrr!" Sheree growled.

Brendon knocked on her door and opened it without waiting for a response. "Thanks for the wakeup call!" he told her, running down the stairs into the living room, the sound of his steps echoing through the house, which somehow seemed louder than usual, the creaking seeming to get worse in cold weather.

"Oh, that's right, Santa came last night," Sheree said unenthusiastically as she pushed off her covers and walked downstairs to see what the big jolly elf had brought Brendon. Even though they had lived in the house for months, it still made Sheree just as scared as she was the first day they moved in. Of course, the singing voice threatening to kill everyone she loved didn't help either. Carefully descending the stairs, cautious about her every step, she didn't want a repeat of the time she tumbled down them after falling off the handrail, which suddenly had three new posts that she couldn't remember being there the day before. Why she was doing this was beyond her, since she'd run up and down those steps numerous times after that without incident. Hurrying over to the living room where the lighted tree and the hoary fireplace were, she figured that Brendon was in there already playing with his presents from Santa Claus. But when she entered the room, it was empty, the light from the Christmas tree casting eerie shadows on the stair wall.

Where did he go? Sheree wondered, looking around the open living area to see if she could find him. Turning around, she saw the light was on in the kitchen. *That wasn't on when I came down, was it?* Brushing off the thought, she walked over to the kitchen. *Maybe Mom or Dad woke up too. Or else…*

Or else what? Was there someone else in the house?

Entering the kitchen, there didn't seem to be anyone in there either. Scanning the room, her eyes fixed on a card that had SHEREE written on the front with a teal crayon on the old Formica countertop.

"Oh how sweet, Brendon made me a card," Sheree said aloud. "Damn, he's got sloppy handwriting, doesn't he?" she said as she opened the card, gasping when she read the words written inside.

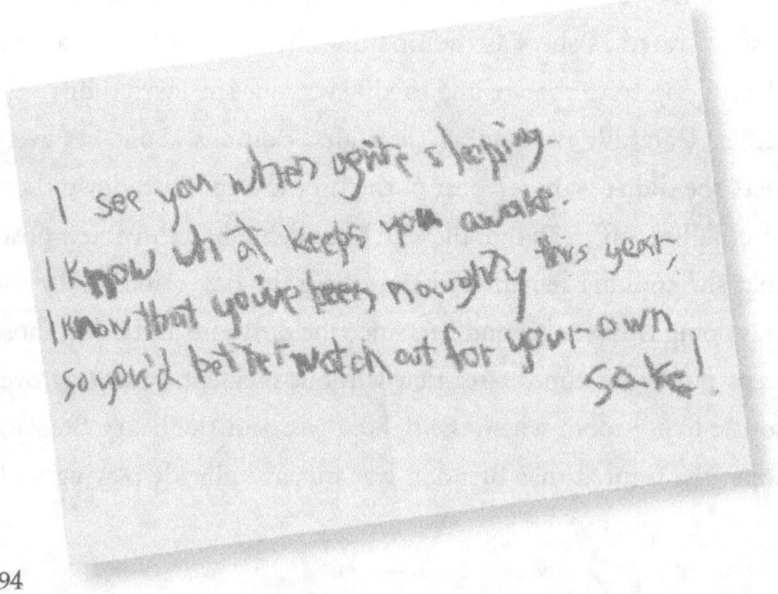

She held the note in her trembling hands.

It was written in red crayon… blood red.

The note was getting heavy

Heavier and heavier the longer she held it in her hands.

So heavy she could barely hold onto it any longer.

It was almost as heavy as a bowling ball.

"Sheree?"

Turning to see who spoke, she saw it was Brendon. "Oh Brendon, you scared me," she said relieved, putting her hand to her chest to steady her breath. Looking down to his hands, she noticed that he was flashing a large knife.

Her eyes widened with fear.

Her body quivering.

Her feet felt like they were glued to the floor.

"Brendon? Why?" Sheree asked with trembling lips.

Looking at his sister with a confused expression, he let out a, "Huh?"

"Why do you want to kill me? Have I really been that mean to you?" she asked, trying to be brave, trying not to show her fear.

"What are you talking about? I was just trying to open this bag of Oreo's. They make the bags so hard to open you know."

Still frightened from the note, she found that her whole body was trembling. Why did someone want to scare her so bad? What did she do to deserve this? Should she really have to go through this torment in the most confusing years of her life?

"Why are you using a knife? Don't you think that's a little dangerous?" she asked, trying as best as she could to pull herself together.

Looking up at his sister, Brendon said, "The knife's not for the bag. It's for you."

He walked closer to her, carrying the knife in one hand and the bag of Oreo's in the other.

Closer and closer.

This is it, Sheree. Think fast.

But it was too late, Brendon plunged the knife into his sister, an evil smile sneering over his round face as it slid into her like room temperature butter.

Did the knife go in? I don't even feel it.

Turning her gaze down, she saw that the knife was in her stomach, Brendon's hand twisting it further into her, his face all screwed up as he continued.

I don't feel anything, she thought, suddenly feeling weak.

Finally, Brendon pulled the knife away from her body, his evil smile back on his face. Taking a look down at the area where the knife was just a second ago, she saw that there wasn't any blood or even a cut in her nightshirt.

Wielding the knife like a pro, Brendon took it and started plunging it into his heart over and over and over. "It's fake you dork! You thought it was real?" Brendon asked, continuing to stab his chest.

Cringing, Sheree shouted, "I told you to never call me a penis!" as she punched his arm, thinking, *How could I be so stupid. Of course it was fake. That was the knife I got him for his birthday.* A forced laugh came out of her.

"Ow, freak. What's that?" Brendon asked, rubbing his sore shoulder with one arm and pointing to the note Sheree had in her hand with his other.

The note.

"Oh this? It's nothing," she told him as she waved the note in the air, a careless look on her face like it was no big deal. "I'm going back to bed, moron. It's too early."

Even though she knew she wasn't going to get any sleep, she walked back up the staircase, the first few steps sounding more like moans of pain than creaking, her hand gliding across the rail during the ascent. *I can't believe myself. This imagination of yours has got to go. Paranoid, party of one. Paranoid, party of one. Your padded rubber room is ready, and your straight jacket is hanging by the door,* she said in her head. After opening the door to her room she went inside, closing it once she was all the way in, taking in a deep breath before plopping herself on top of her bed, back first. Staring at the glittery ceiling, watching the twinkles of light dance across her room in the moonlight, her eyes wandered over to the walls.

Should I paint my room? She wondered. *Maybe a light peach color or lilac? No, dark blue, that'll look really cool with the glitter!* But the idea slipped when she heard the phone ring. Without much thought, she reached over to the floor and picked it up and said into the receiver, "Hello?"

Nothing.

Silence.

"Helloooo?" Sheree repeated.

Still nothing.

C-C-CLICK…

"Oh well, must be a wrong number," she said to herself, placing the phone back onto her nightstand, a surprising yawn escaping her mouth. *Huh, maybe I will get some sleep after all,* she thought as her eyes finally closed, falling fast asleep.

"I hate my hair!" Sheree screamed as she tried to brush out the snarls in her flowing golden hair, ferociously tugging at the stubborn locks. "I knew I should've gotten a perm after I colored it!" She couldn't believe those words actually came out of her mouth, hoping nobody was just outside the bathroom listening in on her conversation with herself and be able to use them as weapons.

It was early Christmas night and all of her relatives were going to be coming to the Hollins house for Christmas dinner and to open presents. Sheree's father's parents were there all day as well, Grandma Hollins helping her mother fix dinner while Grandpa Hollins sat in the corner rocking chair in the living room next to the Christmas tree and silently drinking cheap beer in a can. When her mother's parents arrived at about two o'clock, everything was pretty much under control, with the exception of Sheree, who was still getting ready. For some reason or another, Sheree had to make sure that she looked absolutely perfect, always wanting to look great whenever anyone was coming over, especially family. And this was one of those days that her hair didn't feel like behaving. It wouldn't stay in position. It wouldn't respond to the hairspray, no matter how much she used. She ended up washing her hair twice to get it all out.

There was a knock at the door then a ring of the doorbell, and Sheree could hear her Uncle John and Aunt Jody talking and being greeted by her parents. Little John and Little Jody, their twin son and daughter, were screaming joyously as they spotted their grandparents and all the presents under the tree.

"That's it! I don't care what my hair looks like. I'm not going to mess with it any longer," she declared, looking at her reflection in the mirror. "Hmm, I actually like it like this," she said, observing her hair. It made her look absolutely adorable the way it was carelessly tossed to one side. Satisfied, she left her hair the way it was and went downstairs to say hello to her family.

Aunt Gina must be here, Sheree thought, knowing it had to be Gina because of the uproarious laughter that exploded from the living room. Gina was the family joker. It was hard to believe that Aunt Gina was a part of their family and Sheree always wondered if she was adopted. The rest of her mom's side was thin and tall, and Gina was short and fat. A jolly three hundred fifty pound woman whose exuberance was unmatched by anyone else she knew. Then again, she looked exactly like a stretched out version of her mother, so she probably was blood after all.

"Hi everyone!" Sheree shouted with a wide smile at the bottom of the staircase.

The house went silent as all heads turned toward Sheree.

I hate it when everybody turns their attention to me, it makes me feel nervous. Oh, who am I kidding, I love it! she thought, throwing her hands into the air and striking a pose as everyone said, "Sheree!"

The rest of the night went by fairly smooth. Uncle Rick chowed down on the turkey and the pork n' beans. Aunt Tami spilled red wine all over her snow-white blouse. Cousin Tommy ran into the wall and made his nose bleed. Uncle Billy and Uncle Jack had a long conversation with Brendon about stuff. And Grandma Lowell's skirt accidentally fell off in the middle of the room while she was talking to a group of people. So far, everything was going well.

"Ho ho ho!" Sheree heard from the other side of the large living room.

Richie's Santa again this year, I see, Sheree noted.

Her cousin was dressed in an oversized Santa outfit that obviously made him a fake, but the kids didn't care, they thought he was the genuine article. Half the room was piled with Christmas gifts, big ones, small ones and some the size of your head, and plenty of dollar store gift bags too, but the children only seemed interested in what Santa was bringing them at the moment. Patiently waiting for Richie to finish passing out the presents to the younger kids, Sheree sat next to her cousin Kelly as they discussed everything, being that they were closest in age to each other.

"So, do you have a boyfriend?" Kelly asked, adjusting her skirt that she obviously felt uncomfortable wearing.

"No, he died in a car accident a couple months ago," Sheree informed her, surprised by how easy that came out.

Eyes widening, Kelly told her, "I'm sorry! I didn't know. You need to call me more often so I don't blurt out things like that."

Telling her it was all right, Sheree asked back, "So, what about you? Any new man in your life?"

Leaning over to Sheree's ear, Kelly confessed, "No, not a man, but I do have a girlfriend."

"You're gay?!" Sheree shouted unintentionally, as she meant to only think it but her brain didn't listen. Stupid brain.

All eyes were on her again.

"It's Christmas! Isn't everyone gay… and happy?" she asked, hoping they'd buy the fib.

"I'm gay!" she heard her family start to shout in ones and twos at a time.

"We're gay!" Uncle Billy and Uncle Jack said together, both giggling afterwards.

"I'm not!" her cousin Frank announced before stating rather matter-of-factly, "I'm an effeminate heterosexual."

Everyone was still having a laugh at the gay thing when Richie announced he was finished passing out the Santa gifts, telling all the children, "Merry Christmas to all, and to all a good night!" as he walked out the front door, quickly disposing of the outfit into his car. When he came back, he asked, looking at all the kids playing with their presents, "Oh man, did I miss Santa Claus again?"

"He was just here, I swear to God!" Little John told him, running over to the front door and opening it. "He might still be out there. You didn't see him?"

"Well, I did see a sleigh with eight tiny reindeer and, oh my, that must have been him! I did miss him again. Shucks! Oh well, maybe next year, right?" he asked Little John.

Rolling his eyes at his older cousin, Little John said, "Yeah, if you could get your butt here earlier you might!" before he ran over to the rest of the kids his age, awaiting the rest of the presents to be passed out.

A vote was taken and it was decided that all the little kids would be in charge of passing out the presents.

"Yay, I don't have to pass out this year!" Sheree squealed with delight.

But before she knew it, she was being asked to help pass the presents out with the little ones because they were being too slow… and having trouble reading the names… and complaining about finding their own presents and not being able to open them right away. It was about fifteen minutes later when she finally got to open her gifts. Violently ripping open all of the presents that had her name on them way too fast, she didn't even take the time to see whom they were from. All her patience seemed to have vanished while she waited for her cousin Richie to give all the younger grandkids Santa presents.

More! I must have more! she yelled in her mind, hoping this time her thoughts stayed in her head.

But there weren't any more. All her presents were opened. There was nothing left for her.

"Oh well," she said aloud. *I guess that I can search through the stuff that I've already opened and find out what's from who so I can thank them.*

As she rummaged over the piles of paper that were thrown on top of her gifts, she was looking at a gift tag for a name of who her neon yellow biking shorts were from (since they obviously knew nothing about her, let alone the fact that she didn't have a bike), when she saw an unopened present lying under the pile.

Hmm, I must've missed one.

Grasping hold of the small box, she looked for a gift tag. There wasn't one. Carefully, she unwrapped the paper from the miniature box and pulled off the top of it. There was a note inside, in the same blood red crayon as the one she got earlier that morning.

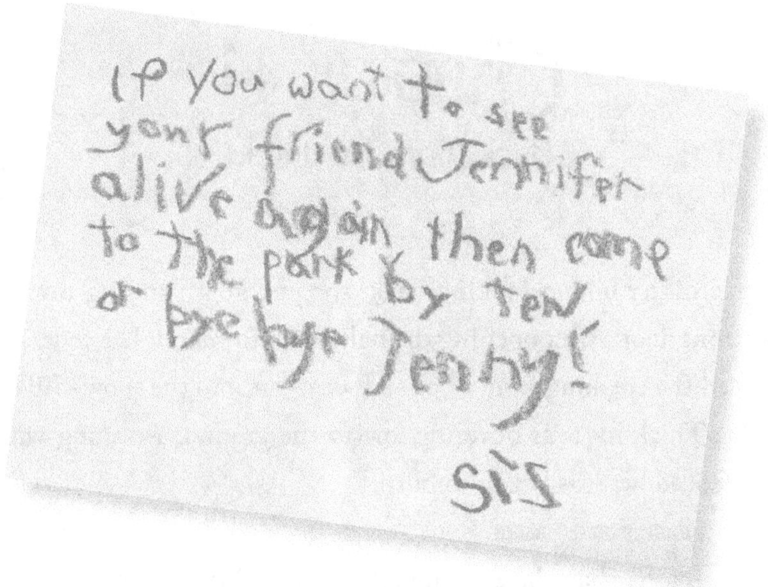

"Oh no!" Sheree said aloud. "I've get to get out of here!" Scrambling to her feet she ran across the room toward the coat closet.

"You're not leaving this house young lady!" her dad called over the crowd of people, nearly losing grip on the bottle of thick dark beer he was drinking. "It's Christmas!"

"I have to go!" Sheree insisted. "I know who the evil is. It's Kayla!"

Chapter 14
Back from the Dead

Sheree didn't bother looking back, she just kept running toward the front door. After opening the hall closet to get out her coat, she opened the creaking front door and went out into the snow-chilled night. Thick fog was hovering low to the ground. Running with great speed her legs began to burn.

Faster and Faster.

Faster than she ever thought she could run. From the front porch, she could hear her father call out to her, but she didn't care. Jennifer's life was in danger and she had to save her.

CRUNCH! CRUNCH! CRUNCH!

The virgin snow crushed under Sheree's feet as she ran, no longer sounding like cornflakes but brittle bones. The ebony black mini skirt that she was wearing made it hard for her to run. At least she decided against heals! Steam was shooting out of her nose and mouth. *Only a couple hundred yards to go. Don't worry, Jen, I'm coming.*

Her head felt like it was going to fall off, her temples throbbing. The park was somewhat lit by the nearby streetlights. Looking at her watch, she saw the time: 9:31.

Where are they? Sheree asked herself, trying to look through the dense fog, the streetlight bouncing off of it, making it appear iridescent.

"Sheree!" Jennifer yelled at the top of her lungs.

Turning toward the direction the voice was coming from, Sheree saw her friend just standing there, another figure next to her. It was green or blue-green, Sheree couldn't tell what it was because of her distance; it just looked like a glowing orb of light without any definition.

"She…" Jennifer started, but was suddenly lifted then thrown to the ground.

"What the…?" Sheree said, not believing her eyes, watching as Jennifer's body was jerked up and tossed like it was nothing when the glowing light spoke.

"Oh Sheree?" a wicked voice said.

It was evil.

So evil; witch-like, child-like, and very throaty. And obviously the same voice that had been haunting her, singing to her its twisted little lullaby over the past few months since moving into the old house on Song's End.

The specter and Jennifer kept getting closer and closer, but they weren't moving. Not even realizing it, Sheree had started walking toward them, somehow entranced by an evil force.

"Kayla? Is that you?" Sheree asked, continuing to walk toward them, thankful she wasn't under complete control of the phantom that had driven so much fear and anger into her.

Its eyes were blank.

Empty.

"Of course it's me you fool!" it shrieked.

Trying to escape, Jennifer got up and made a run for it, but Kayla put a curse on her, making her unable to move; unable to break free and run for help; unable to do anything but watch.

The evil glowing teal light morphed into a little girl, wearing a blue gingham dress and tights with church shoes, her pale yellow hair in pigtails. It was the Kayla that Sheree knew, the innocent one. The one who was killed. Although she hated wearing dresses, so why she would decide to wear one now that she was dead was mindboggling to her. Until she realized it was the outfit she was buried in. Although it was closed casket due to the amount of damage her body had taken, their mother insisted she wear her Sunday best.

"C'mon, Jennifer. Let's go play," four-year-old Kayla said, grabbing Jennifer's arm and dragging her over to the swings.

Completely spellbound, Jennifer looked like she had no control over what was happening. No control over anything. Shock.

"Stay away from her!" Sheree yelled out, but Kayla ignored her.

"We can play on the swings. Go ahead. I'll push you really high!"

Running closer to them, Sheree suddenly realized her body was freezing from the cold, even though she was wearing the heavy purple sweater and her down jacket. *Damn nylons! Why can't you be warm too?*

The snow on the swing flew off with a magical blow from Kayla. Giving Jennifer a shove, she landed precisely on the seat of the swing. "Really high!" Kayla repeated with a childish voice, as she pushed Jennifer once, sending her flying toward the sky.

"Hold on, Jen!" Sheree screamed, watching her friend suffer. "Just hold on!"

"Shut up!" a frightening voice screamed, her face twisted and corrupt. It quickly changed back to the small voice, her face untainted again. "You want to go higher? Okay."

"Why do you have such a vengeance against me? What have I done to you?" Sheree asked bravely.

"What did you do to me?" Kayla interrogated. "You know very well what you did. You killed me!"

"I didn't kill you! You ran into the street and got ran over by a truck!" Sheree told her sister, trying to refresh her memory.

"*You* killed me!" she snapped.

A sickening crunch echoed in the night as Jennifer was thrust forward, somersaulting in the air and landing on her back, her head in the snow and her face showing pain as her long black hair surrounded it like octopus tentacles.

"Leave her alone, Kayla! If it's me you want, then you've got it!" Sheree screamed, hoping her sister would take the offer.

Immediately Kayla's spell on Jennifer was cast off, making her once again able to have free will.

I'll go get help Sheree. You just keep her busy, Sheree heard Jennifer's voice say in her head.

How did I hear that? I'm not a mind reader? "This is weird," Sheree uttered under her breath. *Please hurry back, Jen.*

Don't worry. I will.

"That's it! I'm losing my fucking mind!" Sheree yelled, throwing her hands up to the night sky.

Seizing Sheree's arm, Kayla pulled her into the dark forest, still disguised as the small child but obviously much more powerful than one.

"Where are you taking me?" Sheree asked, watching as the starlit night disappeared behind the tops of the trees in the Ravenwood Forest, and as the earth-hugging fog disappeared beneath their feet.

Kayla didn't answer.

There's nothing in the woods. It's totally empty. The only thing behind it is the cliff...

The cliff.

Could Kayla be taking Sheree to the cliff? Is she planning on throwing Sheree over it, sending her flying to her death?

Propelling the front door open, narrowly missing one of the kids who was playing with his toys next to it, Jennifer burst into the old house on Song's End where Sheree lived, her heart pounding wildly, her lungs out of breath. "Frank!" she yelled, gasping wildly when she found him in the kitchen. "Sheree's in trouble! You have to help her!"

Confused, Mr. Hollins turned around, along with a few other people who all looked at her like she was on crack or something. "Jennifer? What are you talking about? Sheree is right here."

Unable to believe her own eyes, Jennifer couldn't figure out what was going on. There was Sheree; dressed in the black miniskirt and purple sweater she gave her the night before.

"Hi, Jen! Isn't this a surprise? What happened to you, you look like you just saw a ghost?" Sheree asked with mock concern.

A shiver ran up her spine when she heard Sheree talk. Confusion swept through her. *Am I going insane? How could Sheree be at the park and be here at the same time? Unless...* Jennifer stopped herself. "I'm sorry," she said, her cheeks blushing from embarrassment. "I'm just going crazy. Nothing serious."

"You are not!" Sheree said, trying to cheer her up. Putting a comforting arm around Jennifer's shoulder, she told her, scrunching her nose, "Okay, so maybe a little."

Still confused, Jennifer had to make up an excuse for her sudden disturbance that she caused or warn the Hollins family of the evil that resides in their home, but it was like her brain wasn't working properly, nothing wanting to function. There was evil there, right?

"C'mon Jen, I'll walk you to the door," Sheree insisted, leading Jennifer back to the front entry.

"I must be losing it, Sheree. I swore that your sister Kayla was taking you away. But she's dead? How could I have thought that? I feel so stupid," Jennifer told Sheree, shaking her head, trying to make sense of the situation.

Was the park all a vivid nightmare?

Pretending to ignore her, Sheree looked straight ahead. But Jennifer saw that she looked like she was angry, really angry like she was ready to blow any minute.

"Sheree, are you okay?" Jennifer asked sincerely.

Cold eyes looked at her, turning into a fiery blue-green. "That was close, Jennifer."

The words sounded so cruel.

"Huh?"

The door flew open and they walked out.

"Too close."

"Now what are you talking about, Sheree?" Jennifer questioned, completely confused by all that was going on.

The door slammed shut behind them and Sheree's eyes seemed to glow in the dark frigid night. "Stop calling me Sheree! Sheree is dead!" Sheree's doppelgänger screamed, opening the door and slamming it shut again.

Sheree was gone.

Or was it Sheree?

Standing on the front porch, Jennifer was bewildered. "Sheree is dead?" she asked herself. "But how? What is going on? If Sheree is dead then that means that… Oh no! That means that that was Kayla!"

The door flew open again and Kayla walked out, closing the door behind her. Jennifer slowly began to walk backwards, away from what she knew was impossible… a ghost.

"Oh Jennifer?" Kayla called out as Jennifer tried to run away. "Remember that night in the basement?"

Jennifer froze.

The basement.

The burglar.

"Maybe this will trigger your memory," Kayla said calmly as she knocked Jennifer unconscious.

*

"Jennifer, help me!" Sheree screamed.

The voice seemed so far away.

"Heeeeeeeeeeelp!"

"I'm trying! Where are you?" Jennifer asked, running in a forest. Running and running, not knowing where she was going or where she was going to end up. *How could I have doubted you Sheree? I should've known that all the crazy things you were talking about were real! I should've listened and then none of this would be happening right now,* she thought as she ran.

"Help Meeeee! Please somebody help me!"

"Tell me where you are?" Jennifer screamed at the top of her lungs, but Sheree didn't seem to be able to hear her.

Jennifer continued to run, running and running but seeming to get nowhere. The forest so dark, no light penetrating its fortress, she couldn't see where she was going, but kept on running for what seemed like miles.

"Wake up, Jennifer, it almost noon."

Quickly opening her eyes then regretting the decision as the pain nearly rendered her comatose again. Once the pain subsided to the point of tolerability, Jennifer saw her mother at the doorway wearing a pair of leggings and an oversized white sweatshirt with some gaudy gold jewelry plastered wherever it would fit. She was still in her blue jeans and blue sweater and blue sneakers she was wearing on Christmas day.

"Where you disappear to last night when we got home?" Mrs. Hoang interrogated her with a wrathful expression on her stout face.

"You wouldn't believe me if I told you," Jennifer mumbled, sitting up, her legs burning with pain like she had been running all night. Oh wait, she was.

"What you say, I not hear you?"

I said I was kidnapped by a ghost and it tried to kill me. "Oh, I uh, went to Sheree's," Jennifer told her mom. *It's not a complete lie.*

"Pretty golden hair girl?" her mother asked, her face lighting up. "She still not take my offer? Next time tell me where you going so I know, okay?"

"Okay," Jennifer said flatly.

Meanwhile at the Hollins residence, everyone seemed to notice something peculiar was going on with Sheree's doppelgänger, as she seemed too happy all the time, even rejoicing in cleaning up the house after the mess that was made the night before.

"Oh Brendon, where are you?" doppelgänger Sheree queried in a singsong voice.

Walking out of his room, Brendon asked, "What is wrong with you? You've been so cheerful and nice lately. Too cheerful and nice. It's starting to get on my nerves, Sheree. Are you feeling okay?"

Astonished at the accusation that something was wrong with her, doppelgänger Sheree told him, "Yes I'm feeling okay. I feel great! It's great to be alive!"

"What in the world are you talking about?" Brendon asked with his hands on his hips.

"Oh, you wouldn't know how great it is to be alive until you've died. Then it dawns on you how wonderful life is," doppelgänger Sheree told him overdramatically.

"Sheree, Sheree, Sheree," Brendon said, shaking his head. "You are starting to scare me. Do you really expect me to believe any of this when you won't believe that I have multiple personality disorder? Besides, how would you know what it's like to be dead?" Brendon questioned her.

"Do you want to find out what death feels like? Do you want to know how horrible it is? Do you want to know what it feels like to be crushed by a huge truck? All the pain? All the hurt?" doppelgänger Sheree asked with a horrifying voice.

"Mooooooooooooooooooooom!" Brendon shouted, about to run down the stairs.

"Shut up!" doppelgänger Sheree screamed, grabbing him by the arm he fractured only months ago.

"What is wrong with you? You're changing moods so quickly that you're starting to act like me!" he shouted, trying to yank his arm free. He could feel the fracture point start to bend. "What are you, some kind of sicko?"

"A sicko?! Am I some kind of sicko?!" Evil, devilish laughter began spewing from her mouth. "Yes!"

"Ha ha. Good joke," Brendon told her, rolling his eyes at the notion, wishing she would let go of his arm, tears beginning to well up from the pain but not wanting his sister to know that she was indeed hurting him. "Although, that would explain a lot of…"

"It's no joke!" doppelgänger Sheree yelled, interrupting him. "I always thought it would be nice to have a little brother, someone to play with and blame things on and do evil deeds for me. But I was wrong! Oh, was I ever wrong. You say I'm sick? I am sick! So very sick! And you're going to see just how twisted I can be!"

Chapter 15
Twisted

Picking Brendon up, they floated from the floor, doppelgänger Sheree's eyes disappearing into the back of her head before she closed them. A second later, she reopened her eyes, a blast of blue-green light darting out like lasers.

Horrified, Brendon was incapable of moving. He couldn't move if he had to, his body was stiff.

Stiff with fear.

"No!" Brendon finally managed, his jaws aching with immense pain as if he broke the wires setting it into the lock position.

As doppelgänger Sheree floated higher into the air, her hands let go of Brendon, keeping him up with her mind now. Possibly she was doing it with the teal lasers shooting out of her eyeballs, like a tractor beam on *Star Trek*.

"Sheree? How are you doing this?" Brendon asked with total confusion, the pain slowly going away.

"It's Kayla, you twerp!" she blared in a raspy other-worldly voice, an angry expression plastering itself behind the glowing teal radiance.

Braving up, Brendon shouted back, "I want my sister back!"

"I am your sister too. Don't you want me?"

"No! You're not my sister! Sheree's my sister! You're just the nasty ghost who's been haunting me since we moved into this house!"

"If it's Sheree you want, then you can have her! I'll throw you where I threw her so you can be together forever!"

Before Brendon knew it, Kayla was taking him outside. The snow made the night sky seem light purple, almost mauve. The wind rustled over him and under him as they flew over the houses along Song's End. Each roof covered in snow; each chimney smoking; each one of them even creepier from a bird's eye point-of-view.

Ravenwood Park was near, and he could see the trees and the play area. Now they were going through the trees, whizzing past them with great speed, flying so close to them that Brendon thought they might hit one. Trying to close his eyes as he watched Kayla swerve them through the dense forest, Brendon wanted desperately to stop. He wanted to go back home, back to the safe house on Song's End and back to his mom and dad. But more than that, he wanted his sister.

"Are you ready to die?" Kayla asked with an innocent voice before breaking out into maniacal laughter.

Gazing up at her bedroom ceiling, Jennifer's mind was on Sheree as she lay on her bed, which was still rumpled up from the night before, the covers only halfway on. Her father came back home just after she was violently woken up by her mother six hours ago, and she was formulating an escape plan. What could she do to save the Hollins family? What did Kayla plan on doing to them? Then Sheree's voice popped into her head, saying, *Jennifer. Come. I know you can hear me. Just like last night. I could hear you talking to me in your mind. I hope you can hear me now. It's freezing. So cold down here.*

Was she imagining it? Or was Sheree really trying to tell Jennifer something? Deciding to take a chance on the impossible, Jennifer closed her eyes and concentrated hard on the voice of her best friend. Suddenly an image struck her and she saw what Sheree saw. She was looking up. Up a rocky wall and it was snowing. Then she looked down to what seemed like a mile long drop under a pair of really cute shoes on a small protruding ledge. *Please come now, Jen. I can feel Kayla. She's near. If she finds out I'm alive, she'll kill me for sure.*

Where was a rock wall? Why did it look so familiar?

"Sheree's at the cliff!" Jennifer thought out loud, springing from her bed.

After grabbing a down coat from her closet, she ran out of the bedroom and through the hall and to the front door. When she opened it, a gust of cold wind greeted her like an old friend, some snow penetrating its way into the entry like an unwelcome solicitor, scattering over the freshly vacuumed carpet making it look like it had dandruff, which caused her normally unresponsive dad to look up from his business reports to find out how the white flakes managed to find their way in.

"Where you go now, Jennifer?" Mrs. Hoang asked her daughter as she walked from the kitchen to the living room with a plate full of Buddha food in her portly hands.

"Out," Jennifer replied, running out the door leaving it wide open.

"Jennifer Nguyen Hoang! Get back here now!" she yelled, but the howling wind drowned out her voice.

The forest was darker than usual, strange sounds and sights everywhere as Jennifer carefully made her way to the other end. Because of the thick crowd of cedars and Douglas fir trees that made up the majority of the forest, with a few maples and oaks and birches spread out here and there, the ground was sheltered from most of the snow. Following the well worn path, she only ran into a few patches of snow, which she was thankful for as she hurried along trying to save her best friend, hoping, praying that she was okay.

⁂

"Are you ready to be rejoined with your precious sister, Brendon?" Kayla asked in her wicked voice, the glowing orbs for eyes displaying all the rage she held inside.

"What have you done to her?" Brendon demanded, surprised by how bold he was considering the circumstances.

"You see the cliff?" the phantom menace asked, her voice showing signs of pleasure.

Widening his eyes with realization, Brendon said quietly, "Yes, I can see it. Why?"

"Do you want to see what's on the bottom of it?"

Cruelness.

Although her face was smiling, her voice was full of anger.

Taking a dry gulp, he asked, voice quivering, "Is Sheree down there?"

"Take a look for yourself! Go on!" Kayla told him, her smile reminding Brendon of The Joker from *Batman* with its unnatural curvature. "Take a nice long look, because you're soon going to be there too!"

Hesitating, he wondered, Did Kayla really kill Sheree? Did she throw her over the cliff?

"Go on! Take a look!" Kayla insisted, her face more perplexing than normal as she lifted Brendon high off the ground and held him over the cliff.

Frightened of what he might see, he held his eyes closed, clenching them with all his might. But a burning desire to see, to know if this ghost was telling the truth, forced him to open them. Floating like a helium balloon tied to a child's wrist over the cliff, he looked down. Sheree wasn't anywhere. There was nothing below him but the bottom of the cliff covered in snow. Looking over to the other side, and following the round shape it took on, Brendon wondered how such a formation came to be. It was almost a perfect circle, and it was a nearly completely vertical drop to the bottom of it, with the exception of a few jutted out platforms spread out on the way down. But they were so sparse that it would take a leap of luck to land on one of them if one accidentally fell over the cliff's edge.

She must be buried under the snow. Poor Sheree.

Small tears began to fall from his face as the thought of Sheree having died such a horrible death, and how he too would suffer the same fate. How could someone kill his sister? Why would they want her dead? What did she do that was so atrocious to Kayla that she had to kill her?

Suddenly, a figure jumped out from the cliff below them, lunging itself towards Kayla, tackling her to the ground. Brendon flew back, landing on the snow-packed rocky ground butt first.

"You're not going to be able to kill anymore, Kayla!" the figure yelled pinning Kayla to the ground, holding down her wrists as the person straddled her abdomen.

But Kayla's powers were too great for the person and she pushed them forward, almost making the individual fall over the deep drop-off of the cliff where the figure had come from. With her hands raised to the sky, Kayla seemed to create lightning. It touched her fingertips at her command. Thunder started pounding. Kayla grew more and more frightening, scarier every second. Then she began to light up, becoming bright enough to illuminate the area around them. The trees were visibly trees, not monsters surrounding them. The cliff was easier to see. Easier to see how deep the drop-off really was.

Looking over to the figure, Brendon's eyes lit up as he did so. "Sheree! You're alive!" Brendon cried as he ran over to his sister, hoping to give her a hug.

"What?! Sheree's alive? That can't be! I killed her! She can't still be alive!" Kayla's voice was filled with uncontrolled anger and confusion.

So much rage.

With a *SWOOSH* of her hands, Kayla caused Brendon to fly toward the ledge, landing on the brink of it. Puckering up her cheeks she started blowing, the blast was so strong that it made Brendon slide over the edge. With all his strength, he held onto a branch of a small tree for dear life.

"Help me!" he cried pathetically.

What could Sheree do? If she tried to help Brendon, her evil twin sister would blow her over the edge, too. She didn't want that to happen, not again. This time she might not be so lucky. Out of nowhere, Sheree's thoughts faded back to the day her sister was run over by the truck, that evil summer day and to all that had happened. All that really happened…

"Do you want to play tea party? We can pretend our aminals are the guests and we're the hosts. We'll make them pay our taxes and do the cleaning," Sheree suggested.

"No. Let's play hidenseek. I like hidenseek. It's fun. You're it!" Kayla yelled running off to hide from her sister.

Cheating, Sheree watched Kayla hide. "…three, four, five, six, ten! Ready or not, here I come!" she said excitedly as she ran over to the bush that she saw Kayla hide behind. "You're it! Now you have to be it and I hide!"

"I don't want to play anymore. Let's do something else."

"That's not fair! I always have to be it! Now it's your turn. Go count!"

"NO! I want to play something else!"

Sheree was angry. Very angry. Malice on her mind, she grabbed Kayla's favorite doll, put her arm way behind her back, and then launched it into the road.

"Casey!" Kayla cried as she watched her only friend fly helplessly into the middle of the road landing face down, limbs sprawled out in an unnatural way. "Go get her!"

"NO! You go get her! She's your doll, not mine," Sheree told her sister bitterly, arms folded across her chest and a bitter pout plastered across her face.

"I'm telling Mommy on you!" Kayla screamed.

"Go ahead! I don't care!" Sheree shouted, stomping off to grab her stuffed animal friends from her room, informing their babysitter that they were going to have a tea party and Kayla wasn't invited, but she was obviously too involved in the conversation she was having with the person on the other end of the phone to hear what she had said.

Kayla looked at her doll, her helpless Casey doll, stranded in the middle of the street. Looking behind her, she saw Sheree was already in the middle of setting up her tea party.

"Please Sheree, go get her. Someone will kill her if you don't!" she pleaded.

Ignoring Kayla's request, Sheree asked her tea party guests if they'd like more tea, and they responded by Sheree speaking for all of them in a different voice. Upset by her sister's cruelty, Kayla knocked over a teddy bear and ran over to the street side of the yard. Knowing that she had to go save her or somebody would smash her with their car, she turned around and glared at Sheree with an evil stare. Turning back around, her little feet trotted out into the road and went to the middle of it where her dolly was. "Are you okay? Did mean Sheree give you an ouchie? Mommy will make it all better, Casey. Don't cry, Mommy's here." She gave the doll a kiss and hugged it to make it feel better.

Her eyes were closed.

A semi-truck sped down the road, heading straight towards Kayla.

HONK! HONK!

Looking up, Kayla's face filled with horror. The truck's brakes could be heard for blocks. But they weren't fast enough. Not fast enough to save her young life.

"I can see that it's going to take more than one time to kill you, Sheree!" Kayla yelled, staring at her with vacant eyes, her body still glowing teal and causing lightning and thunder to strike. "This is it, Sheree. I am finally going to pay you back for killing me." Kayla crept closer to Sheree. Closer and closer until she was close enough to touch her. As she lifted her hands, Sheree rose with them while Kayla mumbled a few foreign words.

What is she saying? Sheree wondered, looking down to the ground. *I wish I was down there. I wish my feet were safely on the ground.* Then, mustering up the courage to speak, she asked, "Why did you bother haunting me for all those months? Why not just kill me?"

Laughing her incessantly evil laughter, Kayla responded, "You idiot! I needed to feed off your fear and your anger to grow strong enough to take corporeal form! Without it, I'd be nothing more than a phantasm, and not the superhuman being I am now!"

Growing angry, then realizing that Kayla was probably still feeding off of her, she calmed down, taking deep breaths before saying, "And Jeff? Did you kill him too?"

"Of course!" she revealed, taking pride in the fact. "I appeared as a little girl in the middle of the road, not much of a stretch I know, but I got two lives for the price of one that night! I wasn't counting on the car coming from the other direction! Do you have any idea how much power you get from killing? It's incredible!" she screamed, laughing again, the sound piercing the frigid night air like a knife.

Thinking about what she was going to do next, she suddenly realized something. "If it gave you so much power, why did you disappear for two months after it happened?"

The laughter stopped and Kayla turned to look at her. "Souls don't always like to relinquish themselves to the abyss… or to subordination. God may be all-powerful in heaven and Satan in hell, but I rule the in between where souls are trapped, the place they end up when heaven won't take them and hell won't accept them. I am purgatory! The other boy was easy to devour, such a weak character. But Jeff, he struggled with me as heaven's doors opened up to him, the bright light encasing his soul all the way as I held onto him, trying to consume his as well. Then, as if being pushed by a great force, he was gone and I was falling back toward Earth. It took me those two long months to regain all the power your boyfriend stole from me!"

"He didn't *steal* it from you, God *took* it from you!" Sheree screamed angrily as tears began streaming down her face, their warmness lasting mere seconds before turning ice cold on her cheeks. "What about the basement, was that you who put me in a coma?"

A wicked smile plastered itself on her ghastly face as Kayla informed Sheree, "No, Jennifer knocked you out."

"So she is in on this! How could she? That bitch, she's my best friend!" an angry Sheree shouted, not knowing who to be madder at, Kayla or Jennifer.

"I didn't say that she had much choice in the matter, considering I temporarily was in possession of her body at the time. Once I had you unconscious, I just walked her over to the wall and thrust her head into it. Fun times, that night." The Joker smile never wavered as she spoke.

"But, but…"

"Boring! I'm ending this conversation!" Kayla declared. "I must continue my work, there is only a short time left," she said, resuming her chanting in words Sheree had never heard before.

Thinking back, Sheree remembered the conversation with her mother where she told her about Kayla talking to herself in a weird language. The crows feet and frogs eyes and wild sage, and wondered if there was some truth to what she told her, even though she insisted she was just pulling a joke on her.

"Heeeeeeeeeelp!" she shouted, twisting in every direction, hoping someone was in one of them. *Brendon! I forgot about Brendon!* "Don't worry, I'll save you," she said, looking in his direction. *Somehow.*

"Get away from her!"

Continuing to talk in an unknown language, Kayla seemed unprepared for the interruption. "What are you doing here?" Kayla questioned the party crasher.

Turning her head in the direction of the voice, Sheree saw it was Jennifer.

"I've come to save my friends, so back off, Kayla!" Jennifer warned, her normally cute Asian face full of fury, her jet-black hair trailing behind her as the wind blew her way.

"Then say bye-bye to your friends, because they're going to die! And you're going to join them!" Kayla told her, the evil laughter erupting again from her mouth, surrounding them.

Jennifer, don't worry about me. Go save Brendon. I'll be alright.

"Fine! I hope you enjoy your death, Sheree!" Jennifer yelled.

What?! How could she do that? Sheree wondered, watching as Jennifer disappeared into the woods. *Some friend she turned out to be!*

"Ha! Even your best friend is abandoning you!" Kayla screamed gleefully.

Don't worry Sheree. I'm just getting Kayla off my back. Do you think you can handle her for a few more minutes while I go rescue your brother? Jennifer's voice asked in Sheree's head.

Oh thank God! Yes, but please hurry, Jen.

Don't worry, I will.

Yeah, like last time?

I'll explain later.

As Kayla was busy laughing a maniacal laugh, a figure slowly walked out of the forest, coming out on the side closest to the cliff, and closest to where Brendon was still holding onto the small tree so he wouldn't fall to his death. It was hard for Sheree to tell if it was Jennifer or not, until she got closer to her brother, where the teal light of Kayla bounced off of her. Quietly walking up to him, she tried to help him up, taking his free hand and pulling him enough to grab his other.

Chanting a few more words in the foreign language, Kayla turned to Sheree and told her, "There, it is done."

"What is done, Kayla?" Sheree asked her sister.

Smiling one of her evil smiles, Kayla informed Sheree, "You'll find out soon enough."

Somehow Sheree knew that these were the last minutes of her life, but what could she do? How could she stop Death from taking her short existence away? How?

"You remember my favorite nursery rhyme, don't you Sheree?" Kayla asked twistedly.

Of course. The Itsy Bitsy Spider. *How could I have not put two and two together to spell Kayla? Wait, that doesn't make sense. Goddammit, Sheree! This is not the time to be thinking about tangent shit like that! Especially math tangents!*

Without delay, Kayla began singing her version of the lullaby with her ever-so-devilish set of pipes. Trying to muffle the noise, Sheree put her hands to her ears to stop the sound, but it didn't help much. Kayla's voice was too loud, too overwhelmingly loud.

"The itsy bitsy spider went up the water spout!
Then comes along her sister, trying to shut her out!
But now her sister's gonna die, the rest are good as dead
As the itsy bitsy spider has come to life again!"

"Oh, I wish that racket would stop," Brendon said in a small voice, his hands bleeding from bark scraping against the palms, splinters digging in under his skin.

"Me too, it's hard to concentrate with it," Jennifer whispered, using all her strength to pull him to safety.

"My foot seems to be stuck," Brendon whispered back. "I lodged it into a crack trying to stay up and I can't get it out."

Devising a plan of action, she asked, "Do you think you can get your foot out of your shoe?"

"I'll try," he told her. He kicked and kicked with his other foot trying to get it out, but he couldn't. His shoes were tied too tight; he couldn't loosen them.

"Can you try to get your foot loose by twisting it in another direction maybe?"

Doing as Jennifer suggested, Brendon turned his foot as hard as he could, his ankle straining with pain as he tried to pry his foot loose. Giving it one last pull, it finally broke free.

"Oooof!" he let out, falling flat on his stomach, the heel of his foot hanging out of his shoe.

"Oh no!" Sheree gasped.

Kayla turned around and shouted in an evil tone, "You?! What are you doing here?"

"Wow, déjà vu," Jennifer said mockingly. "Why are you so surprised? Did you honestly think I would leave Sheree and Brendon alone with a psycho? Seriously? I don't think so."

Kayla's anger was building up. Anger beyond what any human has ever felt.

Rage.

Fury.

How could one have so much hatred, so much revulsion and abhorrence toward another person?

"Prepare to die! You all have to die! And I'm going to kill you right now!"

Kayla's face was more contorted now with a loathsome sneer and swimming in wrath.

"Stop!"

Huh? Where did that come from? Sheree thought, wondering if it may have come from her own mouth.

"You're making a big mistake, Kayla."

"So we meet again, Jeffrey."

"Jeff…?" Sheree asked, looking in his direction, not understanding why he was there when he was supposed to be in heaven.

Walking closer to them, Jeff said, "Come with me, Kayla. I'm going to take you somewhere. Somewhere you should've gone a long time ago."

After walking right up to her, he stopped and took her hand. Magically, Kayla changed into a four-year-old again, returning with it her innocence. All the rage and anger and frustration she was portraying only seconds ago disappeared, vanishing without a trace. Slowly, Sheree settled back down to the snow-covered ground.

"Jeff!" Sheree shouted to him.

Turning around, he looked at her and smiled. He was covered in light radiating from within him. Unlike the eerie teal light Kayla was emanating, his was pure and white. There were no words exchanged, just his smile, followed by Sheree's. A moment later, he turned back around and they walked hand in hand, her sister and her boyfriend. A bright light beamed down from above them and Kayla looked up toward it.

"Am I going to heaven with you?" Kayla asked in her small voice.

"Yes Kayla, you are," Jeff told her, swooping her up into his arms.

Holding on tightly, Kayla looked up as they floated into it until the light vanished as if someone just turned it off like a flip of a switch.

Staring at the void where they were, Sheree said, "Thank you again, Jeff. Thank you so much." Hot tears rolled down her cheeks, still smiling. "Everything's going to be all right from now on."

Walking over to her friend, Jennifer gave Sheree a long hug. "You're right, everything's going to turn out fine. We're all going to be okay."

They continued to hug under the starless night, knowing that Kayla was out of their lives for good; knowing that evil was once again out of Ravenwood; knowing that once again, they could feel safe.

Ignorance is bliss.

Making his way toward Jennifer and Sheree, Brendon said, rubbing his stomach in what they both thought was pain, "C'mon, guys. Let's get something to eat. I'm starving!"

Acknowledgements

Okay, so I know I dedicated this book to my deceased grandmother, my wildly successful stepbrother, and my frighteningly understanding husband, but there are a plethora of other people to thank. Mostly teachers. Like my husband. With that being said, I shall attempt to do a few of them justice here.

Tami O'Rourke Tucker was my freshman English teacher who inspired me to become an English teacher myself (which, in full disclosure, I am still in the process of obtaining my degree.) I also was her teacher assistant. As it turns out, and since we have remained in touch for the [cough] past twenty-something years since that English class, it was the only year she taught English. Figures. Still, she's an amazing teacher and an even more amazing woman. She also, when I asked what the best word to use for a girl to tell a boy that he's being a jerk is, said, "Asshole." As a high school kid in the 90s, hearing a teacher cuss opened up a menagerie of possibilities to my then clean writing style. It has only gotten cruder as time passes. Thank you.

Chuck Robinson was both my Junior Honors English and Creative Writing teacher in high school. Even when my writing was crap, he'd encourage me to keep going. Actually, most of what I wrote was crap. Except for this little writing prompt exercise in which he put a pile of dirt in the middle of the classroom and said, "Write about this." I wrote this book's first draft based off that mound of musty loam, surrounding the story entitled "A Gift from the Grave" into a full novel within a few short months my senior year. Alas, the book would take many twists and turns and overhauls before I finally felt it was ready for the public to dissect with delight and rip to shreds with disgust. Still, I owe a great debt to Mr. Robinson and his ability to make a poor white trash student like myself feel like he could accomplish anything if he set his mind to it, and for that I am forever grateful.

Gerard Smith was my Creative Writing professor during my first attempt at going to a community college, and he completely opened my eyes to the wide world of using cuss words. He loved them. He loved saying them. He loved hearing them. He loved seeing them on paper and reading them aloud for the class. Now, for a fairly vernacularly conservative fellow like my innocent nineteen-year-old self just beginning to explore my sexuality with my best friend (now husband), this broadened my horizons beyond my wildest dreams. Here, yet another teacher was encouraging me to utilize the full realm of words at my disposal, not just the ones deemed acceptable by societal norms, and here a wide-eyed boy became a man. Mr. Smith taught me that words have power. Labels have power. Profanity has power. But he also taught me that with power comes great responsibility to make sure that those words are used to convey emotions or mood, not just because they can be used. There aren't enough words to express how fucking thankful I am he entered my life when he did.

Author Bio

Cory Blystone lives in Vancouver, Washington with his husband Greg, their two dogs Chuck and Lucy, cat Dexter, and what remains of their flock of chickens named after *Buffy the Vampire Slayer* characters. When not in school and doing homework, he enjoys writing, drawing, painting, reading, quilting, gardening, making absurd videos for YouTube, reading, rapping, cooking, baking, oh, and reading. He also was the Managing Editor for Clark College's award winning art and literature magazine, *Phoenix*, for the 2015 edition where his hand can be seen on nearly every page. Literally. He drew or wrote every title, and wrote all of the writer's statements for the literary works by hand to give the magazine a personal journal feel. You can check it out at ClarkPhoenix.com.

"Be aggressive! Be, be aggressive!" could be heard throughout the gymnasium at Ravenwood High School as the cheerleading squad shouted the chant in front of hundreds of spectators towards the basketball players, clapping their hands in rhythm. The black shells of the cheerleader uniforms were blazoned with RHS in purple outlined in white, and a stylized version of a crow, the rather unoriginal yet recent replacement mascot of Ravenwood High. Furthermore, the girls wore purple spankies with crows on their asses, which I suppose is better than the original face of Chief Ravenwood, the Native American leader for which the town was named, to which some girls would joke about an old man riding up their ass all day. The male cheerleaders didn't have to be bothered with such indignities, except for the fact that they were male cheerleaders. However, most of the male cheerleader mockery came from opposing teams, as Ravenwood's cheerleading squad was consistently in the top five during regional competitions, making them a source of school pride.

"That's my boyfriend!" Jennifer Hoang shouted excitedly from her seat in the front row of the bleachers to her friends Sheree Hollins and Sky Hawkins, pointing toward a cute blond guy with a perfectly white toothy grin and remarkably clear blue eyes that sparkled like the midday sun on the sea.

"I know, Jen! You've been going out for months!" Sheree shouted back as she pulled her strawberry blond hair behind her ears, and showing off her freshly manicured nails at the same time, making Jennifer twinge with jealousy. "Well, except for that week during winter break that you decided to break up with him."

Sky, while only a few feet from the other two found it difficult to hear them so she had been leaning to one side of her wheelchair, shouted back, "He's hot, Jennifer! Can I have him when you're done?" She was only half joking.

Jennifer gave her a perplexed look. "You do know he's gay, right?"

"What?!" Sky screamed in something that could only be described as in the pitch of a banshee. "Then why are you dating him?"

"Because he's an amazing kisser!" Jennifer said, positively glowing as she continued to stare at her boyfriend and imagining the make-out session they'd be having after the game.

Sheree leaned over towards Sky and said, "Don't try to think about it too long, you'll give yourself an aneurism."

Sky simply flashed a confirmatory grin in acknowledgment. Making herself as comfortable as she could, she continued to watch the game, which, quite honestly, was more fun than she was expecting it to be. Of course, she knew a big part of that was her new friends, her only friends so far at Ravenwood High, who were so easy to get along with and didn't make her feel like a freak for having wheels instead of working legs.

The score was already twenty-one to sixteen at only four minutes into the first quarter, with Chancellor in the lead. Chancellor; the school Sky had to transfer from after the accident that took away her ability to walk and her boyfriend's life, who would be on the opposing team had he not been killed; the school she spent her freshman year and one short month into her sophomore before ending up in a hospital; the school she thought she would graduate from. But all that is part of her past, and now she's a Crow. She recognized all of the Chancellor players and knew many of the people in the bleachers supporting them, however she felt uncomfortable even attempting a hello, let alone a conversation, all thanks to her recent mobility issues.

"Hey, Sky! I think that guy is trying to get your attention," Sheree said, touching her shoulder.

The words broke her out of the trance she had found herself in while reminiscing about her past and contemplating the challenges of her future. Looking in the direction Sheree was pointing, she saw Tom, her boyfriend's best friend waving at her, and gave him a half-hearted smile and matching wave back.

Don't start crying, damn it! Don't do it!

Noticing Sky's eyes start to water, Sheree suggested, "Let's go get something to eat at the snack bar!"

Sky nodded her approval before asking, "Want us to bring you back anything, Jennifer?"

As if she was thinking long and hard, with overly exaggerated expressions on her slightly round yet petite Vietnamese face, Jennifer responded with, "Yeah, I want a hot dog real bad!"

"I wonder why?" Sheree said playfully, pointing toward the male cheerleader eye candy only a few yards away, making Sky chuckle.

Jennifer's face was full of resentment. "Not everything I say has sexual innuendo, you know? Granted, a disproportionate amount is, but not everything!"

As Sky wheeled out of the gym with Sheree by her side, she said, "Thanks. I don't know why, but seeing Tom again just brought out the emotional basket-case in me."

Assuming Tom was the guy waving at Sky, Sheree responded, "After my boyfriend Jeff died, I was a zombie for weeks.

Of course, it didn't help that I'd stare at the graveyard he's buried at every day from my bedroom window."

"Oh, that's healthy!" Sky said with a bizarre laugh, making Sheree cringe slightly as it reminded her of another person's laugh who had caused her so much grief and pain and agony… her twin sister, Kayla.

Kayla, who was taken so young, yet allowed to wander aimlessly as a ghost, haunting her in such nightmarish ways. What would she have done if the roles were reversed, if she had been killed instead? Would she haunt? Would she torment? Would she kill?

"I know we need a hot dog," Sky said, causing Sheree to come back to reality. "I think I will have nachos with extra jalapeños. What do you want?"

"Um, uh…" Sheree fumbled around for words, but seemed

to be having difficulty getting anything out until from somewhere deep inside her, buried and clawing its way out, she said, "Your soul!" with a gravelly voice she knew was not hers.

"Huh?" Sky didn't know if she heard right, but played along anyway. "I don't know if they serve souls here. How about some French fries instead?"

Embarrassed and shocked at what came out of her mouth, Sheree covered it with her hand, her face turning scarlet. "I'm sorry! I have no idea where that came from!"

The volunteer basketball mother behind the counter looked like she was getting annoyed, along with the few people in line behind them. "Is that it, or do you want anything else?" she snapped.

"Yeah, French fries and three Cokes, please!" Sheree said quickly.

Sky turned to Sheree and said quietly, "I drink diet."

Making a gagging noise loud enough for everyone around them to hear, Sheree said back, "Not tonight!"

After paying for the snacks, Sheree grabbed a Coke and the nachos and handed them to Sky before picking up the remaining two drinks, hot dog and fries to take back to the gymnasium. When they returned, the crowd was cheering raucously and it didn't take long to realize why after looking at the scoreboard. Ravenwood was ahead by twelve points. When they got to their seats, Sheree asked Jennifer as she handed her a drink and the hot dog she hadn't realized was naked, "What the hell did we miss?"

"The most amazing two minutes of play I've ever seen!" Jennifer said, squealing with delight. "Oh, thank Buddha you didn't put anything on my hot dog! I almost forgot to tell you plain." Jennifer sat back down, put her Coke next to her, reached into her purse and pulled out a full-size bottle of Sriracha. "I never leave home without it!" she said, grinning goofily at an imaginary camera before squirting the hot sauce onto her hot dog.

It was all too much for Sheree, who just could not let the metaphor continue to go unspoken as she said, "Really? You're putting cock sauce on your hot dog?"

Nearly choking out a laugh with the hot dog firmly lodged into her mouth, Jennifer accidentally spit some of the chili sauce onto Sheree's shirt, cheek, and her left eye. Her eyes were full of apology as she knew she couldn't say anything with the giant bite of hot dog she'd just taken still rather unchewed and not ready for swallowing.

"It burns!" Sheree screamed, dropping her fries into Sky's lap, who quickly grabbed the drink cup from her hand before that also had a chance to spill on her, placed it on the bleacher, opened up a packet of mayonnaise she'd grabbed for the fries (yes, mayonnaise), and held it up to Sheree to place in her left eye to ease the burning, to which Jennifer told her to open a packet of ketchup instead, so Sky did as she said and handed the opened packet to Jennifer, who carefully squeezed its contents onto her friend's left eye. Sheree could feel the fiery stares of a dozen kids around them and shouted, "Seriously, this is more interesting than the game?" as ketchup oozed off her eye, down her cheek, and onto her heather grey zip-up hooded sweatshirt splattered with red.

"Well, in their defense, you did just get shot in the eye with cock sauce at a high school basketball game. It's not like this sort of thing happens everyday!" Jennifer pointed out before bursting into hysterical laughter, which caused Sheree and Sky to do the same.

Taking a napkin from one of the pockets in her hoodie, Sheree wiped off the remaining ketchup from her face and shirt before sitting down, grabbing the French fries which had landed so elegantly into Sky's lap that only one had escaped the confines of the food tray. Sky handed her the packets of mayo and ketchup, including the opened mayo, and Sheree squeezed every last bit from all of them on the fries before taking three at a time and shoving them into her mouth.

As Sheree was busy stuffing her face, she felt a tingling sensation dancing across her tongue. At first she attributed it to possibly getting some of the Sriracha sauce in her mouth, but this wasn't hot, but more like less intensive Pop-Rocks. Brushing it off as just a figment of her imagination, she reached for another handful of fries, but before she could eat them Jennifer grabbed her hand. "What the hell, Jen?"

"Sheree, you need to drop the fries now," Jennifer said quietly, trying to keep calm but showing the fear in her eyes.

Looking at her hand, she saw why.

Spiders.

Lots of spiders.

Little. Black. Spiders.

She dropped the container onto the floor of the gymnasium and saw that they had not only invaded her French fry tray, but were surrounding her feet. Moving about like soldiers marching, Sheree could swear they looked like they were starting to form words. Behind the spiders, the cheerleading squad was forming a Wolf Wall during a timeout, but she and Jennifer couldn't take their eyes off the arachnids, no matter how impressive the stunt was. The audience was in an uproar, many of them getting to their feet to cheer on the cheerleaders, when the double doors leading outside burst open, letting in a ferocious whistling wind that seemed filled with what sounded like faint laughter.

Two loud *THUNKS!* echoed off the walls almost simultaneously. It took a few moments for everyone to realize just what had happened. But after a horrified scream shot out, all eyes were on the cheerleaders. Specifically two cheerleaders, who were on the floor in twisted, mangled, unnatural positions.

Blood.

Lots of blood.

Growing puddles of thick, red blood.

But all Sheree and Jennifer could focus on were the spiders, which were now making their escape through the open doors out into the frigid night. Sky on the other hand, couldn't take her eyes off the broken girls on the floor. Part of her was filled with a great sense of satisfaction, something that surprised her until she thought about it. Those two girls had been so merciless in their bullying, so mean spirited and hateful towards her that she felt no sadness for the awful accident they'd had. Instead, she was thankful for karma.

Suddenly, and with a violent force, Sheree vomited all over the floor, adding partially chewed fries to the mess in front of her. She felt another tickle in her throat, but instinctively swallowed before she could stop herself. She knew that it was one of the spiders, but at this point, her focus was on the two cheerleaders lying on the floor. They looked so awkward, so out of place, so broken, that she had to hold herself back from getting up to put them back together. Like Humpty Dumpty, they'd fallen off the wall. And like Humpty Dumpty, nobody was going to be able to put them back together again.

"They're dead!" Courtney, one of the girls on the squad yelled, collapsing onto the wood floor and causing the chatter all around them to silence.

Sheree turned to her left to find Jennifer hugging Chad, tears streaming down his cheek as he cried in disbelief, "How could this happen?"

Then she turned to her right to find Sky, staring at the dead girls surrounded by pools of blood and their saddened and shocked teammates and parents, with a smile on her face. An evil, pleased smile. It was almost enough to make her throw up again.

How could she be happy two people are dead?

Sky's eyes locked onto Sheree's as she said coldly, "Isn't it a tragedy?" She was still smiling. "They never got to finish the routine… and now they never will."

The room began to spin. Noises began to slur together. The lights got brighter and brighter and brighter until suddenly everything went black.

"Sheree, can you hear me?" she heard. The voice sounded so far away. Her head and right elbow were throbbing with pain. Slowly, she opened her eyes and was flooded with such harsh light she immediately closed them again, hoping that the nightmare that had happened in the gymnasium was just that, a nightmare.

You only wish it were a nightmare, but I guarantee that I am the only nightmare you should fear!

Her eyes shot open, filled with horror as she thought, *She's back!*

I know, another voice said in her head.

And with that, she knew that the psychic connection she had with Jennifer was back; the one that was only made possible by the presence of pure evil. After taking a mere month hiatus off, Kayla was back to haunt them, and she obviously had more power than ever.

Are you happy now? You've gone and read the whole goddamned book from cover to cover. I'm so proud I could cry.

9 780996 694834